METAPHYSICS IN THE MIDWEST

Stories by
Curtis White

METAPHYSICS IN THE MIDWEST

Stories by
Curtis White

Sun & Moon Press
Los Angeles

Copyright © Curtis White, 1988
Cover: *Juggling Cactus in Parnell Ia.*, by Jeff Wilson
Design: Katie Messborn
Acknowledgements
"A Disciplined Life" and "You've Changed" appeared originally in *Fiction International*; "More Crimes Against the People of Illinois" in *Canard Anthology*; "Howdy Doody is Dead" in *American Made* (New York: Fiction Collective, 1986); "Critical Theory" in *Another Chicago Magazine*; and "The Order of Virility" in *Epoch*.
Publication of this book was made possible, in part, through a matching grant from the National Endowment for the Arts and through contributions to the Contemporary Arts Educational Project, Inc.

Thanks to the Illinois State Historical Library and the Kansas State Historical Society for Permission to use the photographs in these stories.
The author also wishes to thank Illinois State University for its generous support.

Library of Congress Cataloging in Publication Data

White, Curtis
  Metaphysics in the Midwest
  I. Title   88-062134

ISBN: 1-55713-045-0
ISBN: 1-55713-044-2 [paper]

New American Fiction Series: 18

10 9 8 7 6 5 4 3 2 1
FIRST EDITION

For my teachers, John Barth and Gayatri Chakravorty Spivak

CONTENTS

Metaphysics in the Midwest	9
The Phantom Limb	34
A Disciplined Life	49
More Crimes Against the People of Illinois	67
You've Changed	88
Howdy Doody Is Dead	107
Critical Theory	127
The Order of Virility	151
Malice	171

Metaphysics in the Midwest

1. The Insulted Brain

"You are God, man. Are you aware of that? You are God."

"I'm not God. I'm just the Commissioner."

"Commissioner Stevie is God. I'm a true believer."

"Okay, okay. Then God's telling you to keep it down or my mom will wake up."

The Commissioner was nervous. He'd been caught at this game once before and the next time would be serious. But a large part of the game was psychological, and it was important to keep the Commissioner's attention scattered. So, if I woke his mom, I was too loud; if I didn't, not loud enough. It was on that wafer, that crescent, that I played.

"Right. We be cool," I said, too loud. "You know what I'm gonna do tonight, man? You're not going to believe it. You are not fucking to believe what I have in mind. I'm gonna bench Clemente and put that big sucker with the thirty-six ounces of salami, Wally Post, man, in right field."

Stevie jumped up. "No fair." Shocked. He was so shocked he didn't even notice his dingle poke out of his flannel PJs. I loved those pajamas. Geronimo, Davy Crockett, Custer, Tonto, the Ranger, man, they were all there.

He wants to tell me what's not fair. "No way, Professor. Wally Post is on the Reds. You have to wait until a trading session, then you can trade Clemente for Post." Then he laughed at me. "If you're that dumb. Like when you pinch hit for Smokey Burgess and had to have skinny Elroy Face do the catching next inning 'cause you forgot that old Smokey was your only catcher."

He rolled around laughing with his hand over his mouth like he was keeping in marbles. "Twelve passed balls in one inning. A league record."

"I'm not dumb. You forget, I *knew* Wally Post. If he connected, it was gone. He's got two in him tonight, I can feel it. Four-baggers. His bat hung down to his knees, not like that guppy you got in front of you there."

That shut him up. He shoved it back into the flannel pocket that Cochise defended, rifle leveled, riding his palomino.

"That's why I went into the Reds organization when I played AAA. I said, when the Post-man retires, it's gonna be me and Robinson and Vada Pinson. I did it all in those days. Run, throw, hit. But then came the leg injuries. I stole so many bases I wore the flesh on my shins right down to the bone. The sky diving this summer opened those old wounds up."

"Are you a sky diver?" the Commissioner asked.

"Not any more. Too old for that. But I'll take you up if you'd like to learn."

"Would I!"

"Say, what time is it? I've got office hours tonight."

He pulled this rattling Big Ben out from under his pillow. "Almost midnight."

"Gee-zus! I've got to git. I'm meeting with students."

Commissioner Stevie scoffed. Where do our children learn to "scoff" in these late days?

"You liar. You're just going to go meet women and leave me to play the whole damn game by myself."

"Stevie, I know how you feel." I did know how he felt. I remembered the uncertainties of boy-being. "You're worried about women. You wonder what you have to do with them. Well, put your fears in the Light. Let the god that is within you help. Ask for something particular. Tell the Whiteness that you'd like to feel comfortable with the idea of women."

"Don't give me that. You're just gonna get drunk."

The Commissioner looked lonely and disappointed. The red-blonde hair on his brow, the freckles, the girl's eyes. He was the very picture of your daughter pouting. But I was already out the window and standing in his mother's geraniums.

"Commissioner, let me leave you with an idea. Something to think about while I'm gone. Imagine a fly in a bottle who wants to know what the bottle looks like."

The pout liquefied. The look of the twelve-year-old Kepler, he who speculates on the gauzy firmament, took its place.

"You mean from the outside?"

"Yeah."

So I didn't feel too bad. He had a knot worthy of Dante to fiddle with and Maury Wills leading off in the top of the first. He was alright.

* * *

"You are God." That's all I have to teach in my course, "Spiritual Growth: Getting All the Way to Infusion." Yes, infusion. Like making tea. Because you've got God inside you and he is needed elsewhere. Forget about what to believe. Believe anything you want. Just let the Smiling One out.

I was sitting in Benito's Downtown Tap having the Italian beef sandwich and a beer, wondering if Laura or Melissa would need help tonight. Benito himself was seeing to the bar responsibilities, which were none too great on Tuesdays. It made for nice quiet office hours.

"Benito, a thought form has a lot of repercussions."

"What?"

"What do you make of the Bears signing Flutie?"

Benito brightened, incandescent, like someone had slapped his face. "Now that was the smartest fucking move they've ever made. That Flutie's a winner. And if McMahon is gonna be hurt all the time you can't blame . . ."

"You're right," I interrupted, "Now if they could just sign the Bronc, Nagurski, to complement Payton, they'd have an offense."

"What?"

At that moment, Laura walked in. I was surprised that it was Laura. She seemed a bit out of place in the class. Hadn't yet found her bearings. Part of the problem was that she seemed to want my class to function like other classes. I thought it would be weeks before she dared to take advantage of my office hours. But what are you going to do with today's students? All a teacher can do is make himself available.

"Laura! Fantastic! Benito, a double rum and coke, please. What would you like, Laura?"

"Nothing, thanks." She set her backpack down on the bar top. She looked young for a returning student, almost like a student-student. So there was something strange in this for me too.

"Come on, Laura. Some white wine?"

"No thanks."

"You know, part of the point of a class like ours is to learn to take a fresh perspective on things."

"You mean things like office hours?"

"Exactly."

"Okay, then how about just a coke."

She was cute with that midwestern plump cuteness. As if Illinois thought girls were like frankfurters. But I'm sure she never had an evil thought, so I liked her. I was glad she'd taken the class.

She took a sip of her coke, pulling it innocently up through the straw.

Then she said something. "Isn't it kind of weird to be having office hours this late at night in a bar? To tell you the truth, I didn't think I could stay awake this long."

"It's not weird for me."

"Oh."

"And after next week's class we won't be meeting at Schroeder Hall either. Courses offered in conjunction with the Metaphysical Frontiers Foundation are customarily held at the homes of those in the study group. It creates an important intimacy among members."

"I didn't realize that, either. I don't know how comfortable I am with that."

There was something about the way Laura moved her lips when she talked that charmed me. They made soft, wet, plopping sounds that had nothing to do with the words she spoke, that were entirely her lips' own language.

"You'll need to get beyond your fears if this course is to be of any use to you."

She shrugged her shoulders with a nice resemblance to what you see people doing.

"I'll give it a try."

Then Melissa walked in. She was a more typical student for my course. Whereas Laura expected a meeting of the Young Hegelians, Melissa came in looking for what I really had to offer: metaphor, self-realization, spiritual growth, good vibrations. However, it is important for me to admit, the one thing I've learned about teaching is that I never know who my best students are. That understanding comes about slowly, over a long period of time, and usually only after I have once again surrendered more of myself, more waxy gouges from my own thigh.

Melissa was thirty-six that semester, but she still had

a young woman's figure. She dressed casually but with some gold jewelry and spangles which pleased me. She was married, had a two-year-old son, and worked in the personnel office of a local K-Mart, a position to which she'd been recently promoted from cashier. Melissa took classes like mine to keep her mind lively. Her husband, Lester, thought it was generous to allow her a few nights to herself. He stayed home with the baby. This was all only months before Melissa joined Alcoholics Anonymous.

"Melissa! Fantastic! Benito, a double rum and coke. Melissa, what can I get for you?"

"Are we going to have a drink?" She laughed loudly. "I think I'm gonna like this class. Just a beer."

"How about a shooter with that beer?"

"A shooter?"

"Yea. A little thimble of the old boyo to give the beer some kick."

"I better not."

"Okay. But timidity is failure in this class. We need to learn to release. To give up our attachments and our fears. What we think we have to lose is usually nothing at all. What we need is the freedom to get 'completely drunk,' in a manner of speaking."

"Yeah, I guess so."

Melissa really wasn't very pretty. Motherhood, marriage, avarice had been working on her face like busy worms. But there was that special little sneaky look in her eyes that said "I want to live," which seemed to her to have something to do with sex. She was one of those women who thinks sex is a conspiracy, an underground. Her sly grin says, "If you'll bring it up, we can talk about cock and pussy all night, and no one will be the wiser."

But it was Laura who spoke first that night. "What is your background, Professor Feeling?"

"Please, call me Bill."

"Bill."

"You mean, why do I get to teach this course instead of Benito here?"

"Yes, I suppose." She giggled and took another nervous sip of her coke, which was already only a runny stain at the base of a stack of ice cubes.

"Ultimately, I get to teach the course because I'm the name on the Kankakee College Continuing Education payroll."

This amused but didn't satisfy her. Melissa, too, looked serious, fun over, as if she thought some of the mysteries might be getting started. "I mean, they must have had a reason for hiring you."

"You want to know about my credentials."

"Yes."

"I have none. You can teach the class, Laura. I'll give you all of my money."

* * *

Of course, eventually I explained that the Metaphysical Frontiers Foundation was related to the Spiritual Frontiers Fellowship which has seventy-three regional organizations in thirty-five states. Through the rituals of meditation, prayer, and group study, members focus on a God who dwells within the souls of men. I began my studies in Evanston in 1977. I came to Kankakee only recently in order to establish a metaphysics study group of my own. I felt the need to help those who might otherwise flounder.

I was still describing my interest in psychic and spiritual experience, in Meher Baba and Madame Blavatsky, when Benito announced last call for drinks.

"Say Benito, you should take my class. Next week we do 'Communication with the Dead'."

"What's that?" he asked, a little angrily.

"Another of my little Pepsis, please. And a shooter for my prize pupil."

"Are we really going to communicate with the dead?" asked Laura, rousing herself for the last time.

"Sure. I mean, we'll try. We'll see if my communicator can put us in touch."

"God. This is too much." She lifted her sea-blue pack up on her shoulder with nearly Buddhist control. She looked gorgeous. I could imagine her as a celestial detail in a Tibetan thangka. She seemed gifted to me, at that moment, in spite of her boredom and her skepticism. Her virtue shone through like the infant Dalai Lama's.

"Is there no one close to you who has gone on to the other side?"

"Yes," she acknowledged, hesitantly. "My father died of a heart attack when I was in high school."

"And wouldn't you like to talk to him again, if you could?"

"Sure."

"We'll try, sweetheart, such things can be done."

A little twist of pain caught her face. Melissa, who'd been listening to all this, said, "Wow. This class is going to be heavy." She threw back her shot, a squeeze of pain of another kind on her face.

As we left, I took Melissa by the elbow. "Do you have a car?"

"A little Honda Civic," she replied.

"Can you give me a ride home?"

"Sure."

"Better yet, would you like to visit the Commissioner?"

"The Commissioner?"

"The Commissioner is God," I said, penetrating the puddle of her blue eyes.

Next thing, I had both hands on the butt of Melissa's blue jeans, pushing her through Stevie's bedroom window. She landed on his bed, all over the Commissioner, in fact, waking and scaring him.

"Oh God, Professor, what are you doing here? What time is it? I'm gonna get in so much trouble."

"Dr. Feeling, there's someone in here. A little boy."

"That's the Commissioner." I turned on his Zorro night light. "How'd the game come out?"

"Dodgers two-zip behind Koufax."

"Shit. What did Post do?"

"I told you, Wally Post could not play."

"You see that mastery, Melissa? That's why he's the Commissioner."

"This is so weird. It's three o'clock in the morning and

I'm sitting with my college professor on a bed with a ten-year-old boy."

"What were you expecting?"

"I don't know. I thought 'going to see the Commissioner' was like 'going to the submarine races'."

"Sorry. Say, get me the box score, Stevie, I want to see who got the big hits."

The Commissioner got out of bed, his pajamas dragging around his girlish hips. "Here, but keep it down or my mom is gonna kill me."

"No sweat. By the way, Commissioner, this is Melissa. She's one of the women you were so worried about. I thought you'd like to meet her."

"Glad to meet you."

"Glad to meet you, Stevie."

We gathered our knees together on the Commissioner's bed, Indian style, like we were kids sitting around a campfire. Or we could have been disciples practicing zazen. Then I said, "You see, she's not so frightening, is she?" Boy, he got embarrassed at that. "Melissa, give the Commissioner a hug."

"Are you kidding?"

"No, that's okay, really. I like her."

"He's got insecurities about girls and I want to help him. Give him a god damn hug."

"Be quiet, Professor!"

"I don't know . . ."

"He's just a god damn little kid, so give him a fucking hug."

Animal paralysis seemed to set in with those two.

"Alright, I'll show you how." I took Stevie's arms, stiff as a little Frankenstein's, and reached for Melissa.

Then there was a huge knocking at the door. Big rattling of the handle.

"Steven! Steven Bruce! What's going on in there? Open this door."

"Nothing, Mom. (Get out of here, you guys.) I'm sleeping."

"It doesn't sound like you're sleeping. Who's in there?"

"No one. It's just me being Vin Scully for my baseball game."

"Let me see you. Open this door."

We were out the window. "Bye Commissioner." Melissa wanted to run (what a nice scene: a middle-aged housewife sprinting from a ten-year-old's bed), but I pulled her up against the house, behind a bush, hoping there would be more. Sure enough, Mrs. Commissioner stuck her head out the window. "Why is this open? It's freezing in here." She had the light on and I liked what I saw, Mom in her glowing nightie. In theosophy, constellations are named after such visions.

2. The Ego as Defined by Its Absence

Although Laura was reluctant to commit herself to the unorthodox education offered by Metaphysics, she had relevant needs and a familiar desperation. Not only had her father died a few years before, but she'd recently gone through a searing divorce. It was one of those affairs in which the woman commits herself headlong but naively, with no self-knowledge—no knowledge period—and then is amazed to see the husband drunk, violent, roaring the family chopper around the duplex at two o'clock in the morning, doing doughnuts on the neighbor's lawn and leaving it up to the wife to explain to furious Mr. and Mrs. Nextdoor. But as wrong as this first life decision is, these spontaneous creatures seem to have an uncanny nose for remedies, although those remedies are chastened and far from immmediate: they get jobs, their own little apartments, they enroll in college. In short, they furnish the void.

This was precisely Laura's situation. She discovered my adult education class in Metaphysics in the same way every other resident of Kankakee had— through a brochure addressed to "Boxholder." Also offered by the "K.J.C. Adult Ed. Prog." were courses on belly dancing, Christmas crafts and psychology. She took Metaphysics because it fit her schedule and appeared more rigorous and academic than the others. Her impression of the class after actually attending a session was that it was perhaps even less rigorous than Christmas crafts, but she came quickly to hope that—beyond my eccentric pedagogy—this might be a course about exactly what she was most troubled by: the absence of meaningfulness in her life. What I wanted to say to her from the very first was yes, yes, yes, that's right.

"Thousands of people die miserable every day for lack of the study I suggest to you." That's what I said to them in week five, ten, twelve, whatever it was, in Laura's little apartment. "To avoid desolation—what after all our death culture has most to offer—and discover real knowledge, you must move from a merely customary awareness of material existence to a plane of true intuition at which love and knowledge may be actualized."

Laura and Melissa never did figure how to respond to such proclamations. They stared like a couple of stunned carp, with no notion of what sort of response they might appropriately risk. At least, on that night, Melissa was willing to say something.

"I have a lot of trouble knowing what to say about this stuff. I guess I feel inadequate. You and the books we read are too much smarter than I am. I'm sure it has to do with my self-image problem."

"Melissa, consider the virus. What is it? A genetic code wrapped in a protein shield. And what does it want? It wants every other living cell to devote itself to reproducing the virus's own vainglorious, naughty-sneaky genetic message. It's like a combination lock with Ghengis Khan's will to power. So, the virus has no self-image problem. But is what we're after here the willingness to assert oneself as infinitely desirable? It's entirely the wrong question. The real problem is to get beyond issues of personal worth, and on to the issue of making the God-unit, fragmented as it now is, whole again."

"I think I see what you mean," said Laura, almost unaware that she was saying anything. More like she was talking to herself.

"You're talking about a kind of 'availability'."

"Yes."

"A kind of availability and a denial of even minimal

engagements with trivial preoccupations."

A star was born. Melissa, on the other side, looked crestfallen, confused and marooned. I didn't want Laura's breakthrough to be Melissa's falling away, so I stood and abruptly dismissed class. That is, suggested that Melissa and I should be going.

"I've got to meet the Commissioner yet this evening."

"The Commissioner?" asked Laura. "Who's that?"

"It's a funny thing to explain, actually. When I first moved to town about two years ago, I read an ad in the classifieds by a young boy who was looking for someone to form a statistical baseball league with. I responded, we became friends and now on several nights each week we get together to play the '62 Giants against the '69 Mets. Or the '63 Dodgers against the '75 Reds. There's something so beautiful about the way the game insists: time is nothing, identity is undecidable, only the Event matters, and it is universal and perfect regardless of how it comes out."

"Oh. That is strange, but kind of nice I guess. That you have a friendship with a little boy."

"He's basically without a proper father."

"Well then it's very nice. But his mother sure lets him stay up late. It's almost eleven now."

"Yes, doesn't she?"

"Does that mean that there won't be time for a beer this evening?" Melissa squeaked desperately, her aura throbbing with fear of abandonment.

"There's always time for a little beer," I counseled.

"Then can you drop me off at the Commissioner's?"
"Love to."

Much later that evening, in the top of the fifth, I squatted on the Commissioner's bed giggling and staring at the wall. Elston Howard had just hit one into the gap and Kubek, Mantle, and Maris had skipped giddily to the plate making it a 7-1 ballgame. The Commissioner was pissed off.

"You're not even paying attention. It's not fun for me to win if you don't care if you lose."

He was right. I was too amused to concentrate that night.

He continued. "And why did you pick the '64 Cubbies against the '62 Yankees? And pinch hit for Ernie Banks with men on in the fourth? It's stupid."

"I had a hunch."

"Don Zimmer for the great Ernie Banks is not a hunch."

The kid was right and ordinarily I'd have been kicking myself. But I was thinking about the conversation Melissa and Laura would be having the next day. Melissa was surely going to tell all, and who would be more impressed than Laura?

* * *

"Laura, I've got to tell you what happened last night."

"Last night? What?" Laura a little afraid, a little depressed.

"You know I went out with Professor Feeling for a beer

after class and then I drove him over to the Commissioner's. Boy, is that arrangement weird, but that's another story. Anyway, I stopped the car a few houses down from where I should have. I admit, I started it."

"Started what?" Panic.

"I gave him that kiss-me look."

"Oh God."

"So we kissed for a few minutes and then he told me to take off all my clothes. Well, you know his manner, I couldn't say no. It was so exciting. He wouldn't even let me leave my socks on. Right in the middle of the street, practically. And then . . . "

"And then?"

"Maybe I shouldn't tell the rest. It might not be fair to Willie."

"Willie? God damn you, don't stop, finish the story." Something real in that urgency.

"It sounds almost too strange to say, now that I think about it. Maybe I should be ashamed."

"What?"

"He introduced me to a friend of his, 'Shy Bob.' Laura, he carries a vibrator with him in that old leather briefcase. He said Bob's friends just call him Buzz."

3. The Wisdom Event

"So you guys are lovers now?"

"Well," completely pleased with herself, "You might say."

That's how we concluded that incredible conversation. I was depressed, and I was upset about being depressed. I seemed to care about something in this. I had to admit that, once again, I had given myself over to what Professor Feeling called the "torment of hope." And now I was obliged to see that I not only hoped for wisdom or at least some kind of self-knowledge through our study, but I hoped for something from Feeling himself. I was jealous. I felt a failure. And what the hell kind of horrible person was Melissa anyway? She had a husband and a little boy! And doing it in the street like a slut with that porn shop sex toy. I was disgusted.

I had to talk to Professor Feeling. So, I called him and asked if I could come over to get his comments on the journal I'd been keeping.

"Come in, Laura."

He hadn't gotten up to greet me. When I opened his door, he was sitting in the lotus position on a kitchen chair—apparently the only piece of furniture in the apartment—with a tumbler of water at his side. Through our talk he never opened his eyes and only occasionally drank from his glass.

"Welcome. Have a seat." He motioned to a squat meditation cushion on the floor before him.

"I'm sorry to interrupt you, Professor." I was. I was now completely confused about my motives. Really, all I wanted to say was "How could you?" But how could he what? Have a sex life? Prefer Melissa? Own a vibrator? Live without me?

"No problem. I'm just in middle intensity meditation. If you don't mind if I keep my eyes closed, we can talk."

"That's fine."

"Then why don't you just read to me from your journal."

I started reading one of the exercises he had assigned us, about visualizing the body of a giant: "His arteries are soft and elastic and at first I feel a little confined, but when I allow myself to flow, stream with the little blood balloons, I realize that even here in the most constricted place in the giant's body I am in infinite space, free to rise, expand, like smoke infusing the universe." My tongue clucked along, and I soon lost all contact with what I was reading. The words spilled like gibberish. I might have imagined that the Professor and I were sharing a mystic moment, that our thoughts were one, except that when I looked up to see the glow of similar recognition in the Professor's eyes, I saw instead that he was now in very deep meditation indeed. He was asleep. So much for psychic oneness. It was then that I saw, propped behind him up against a wall, his worn leather briefcase. I had to look. I crept to the briefcase and, one item at a time, removed:

an issue of *The Bill James Baseball Abstract*

an empty half-pint of Jose Cuervo

a small stuffed toy parrot

thirteen Bic pens, marked "Property of Kankakee Junior College"

a dozen pages of confused notes

a wine glass

a bottle of Advil

a frisbee

Space, Time, Knowledge by Tartang Tulku

and a nightlight with a picture of Zorro on it
But no Shy Bob vibrator.

"Good night, Laura."

I turned to see Professor Feeling fall from his seat and land on his face. For the first time I noticed the smell of alcohol. The now empty tumbler was still pungent with gin.

I found a blanket, covered him there on the floor, and left.

* * *

Two nights later I called Professor Feeling again. I had decided that he was clearly no guru, but he was nonetheless unlike any other man in the midwest. That much was easy to say. It was true that he had a drinking problem that I didn't understand, but a stable relationship with someone who really cared for him would surely help. And he had something to give me, strange though that something often was. I would tell him how I felt.

But he didn't answer his phone. I was afraid he was with Melissa, so I called her. Lester answered.

"She's not home now. Who is this, please?"

"This is a friend of hers. Laura Harper."

"You're in the evening class with her, aren't you? With that psycho?"

"Yes, I am. What do you mean psycho?"

"I mean lunatic. Would you like to know where I'm going right now? With our little boy in my arms? I'm going down to City Hall to bail her out of jail. She and that son of a bitch have been arrested."

"Oh no."

"Breaking and entering, sexual misconduct with a minor, drunk and disorderly. That fucker has ruined my life."

"I'm sorry. I'm so sorry."

"Listen, I've got to go."

"But just a minute. Is Professor Feeling in jail too?"

"I was told he'd been taken to the psycho hold at the hospital."

"So he's at Mt. Mercy."

"I think so."

"Thank you. And I hope things turn out okay."

* * *

It was the next morning before I was allowed to speak with him. But first I talked with Dr. Simon Able, chief of staff in psychiatry.

"Would you like to know what happened, Miss Harper?"

"Yes, please."

He was serious about this and not even friendly with me. As if somehow my desire to talk to the poor guy implicated me.

"The police report indicates that at around ten p.m. last evening the police received a phone call from a Mrs. Eileen Warden with a burglary-in-progress complaint. The police arrived in moments and were directed by Mrs. Warden to her son's room. The door was locked and the police forced entry. What they found was this: your so-called professor was drunk and unconscious on the boy's floor. Your friend Melissa was found similarly intoxicated, in partial undress, sitting on the bed with the boy. She could provide no reasonable excuse for her presence or her state, so she was arrested under suspicion of a number of things including child molesting."

"She wouldn't do that," I protested, "she has a little boy of her own."

"I can't speak for her, but I can tell you, as a result of my own examination, that Feeling is a disturbed and potentially dangerous man."

"You don't know him. He's just different."

"Miss Harper," more than a little contempt in the way he said that, "This guy has suffered major insult to a number of important organs due to his alcoholism. Not least among these organs is his brain. His liver has a lethal resemblance to a puff fish, and that's not to be ignored, but his brain, his brain . . ."

The appropriate comparison was testing him.

"Pudding. Tapioca pudding. Just lumpy enough to allow the circuitry to bump into transmission now and then, but generally much impaired."

"Listen. I'd just like to speak to him."

"Of course you may."

The Professor was wide awake and quite calm in bed.
"Laura! Fantastic!"
"Hello, Professor Feeling."
"What can I offer you? Grapefruit sections? Oatmeal?

Java? I don't have any brandy for the coffee, I'm sorry to say."

"That's alright. I don't want anything."

"So what brings you here?"

"I've come to see you, obviously. It's not like you could come to see me. Some terrible things happened to you last night."

"Like what?"

"You were arrested and so was Melissa."

"Oh, she'll be okay. And I'll be out of here shortly. I just need to talk to a few people."

"I don't think you understand. You're under arrest for burglary and child molesting."

"Oh that!" He laughed. "Of course, the Commissioner let us in. And what interest would I or Melissa have in Stevie sexually? That part's really funny."

"I was told that Melissa was undressed."

"All they saw was her blouse was undone. Big deal. Stevie's old enough he needs to know and accept as unremarkable that women are different. It's nothing his mother would ever tell him. And I didn't want him to grow up frightened and obsessed by those differences. As it is, we were probably too late. He said it looked like the face of a sad monkey."

"What are you talking about?"

"I'm saying I love the Commissioner and I've done him no harm."

"Dr. Able says he'll need several years with a good child psychologist."

Just a moment of doubt and dread, perhaps. "No.

That's false. He already understands more than any of them. When they're done, they'll admit that."

"Professor, child molesting is serious business. You are likely to go to jail."

"I spent a month in a Cong cage in Nam up to my neck in putrid swamp water. They pissed on my head for fun."

"I don't believe that."

"And besides the Commissioner has already begun work on a benefit concert for me. This is just like the Dead bust in New Orleans. A frame-up. Rock stars are going to be there—Peter Townsend, man, and Sting and Paul McCartney—and baseball greats, too, like Mays and Roger Maris. Whitey Ford if he can get away from some commitments. These people are in my corner, Laura."

"None of this can be true."

"Can you see McCartney and Stan Musial singing 'Fool on the Hill' for me?"

To that I said nothing.

"You look sad, Laura."

"I am sad."

"Why?"

"I feel disappointed."

"You know, the most beautiful thing that ever happened for Stevie and me in our baseball game was one night through a peculiar and rare combination of rolls the game was rained out in the third inning. Were we ever excited. Imagine, a rain-out! We climbed out the window together and sat on the curb in front of his house and Stevie had his first warm beer and the moon was there and cars rolled by ecstatic. I told you, Laura, the Event is universal and perfect no matter how it turns out."

* * *

I didn't feel like doing anything with the rest of the day, so I went home and turned on the TV. I watched the episode of *I Love Lucy* where she gets caught in Richard Widmark's den hiding beneath a grizzly bear skin. At the moment where Ricky and Widmark stand above her—she sunk in the stink of that hide, peeping up from under its jaw like something just eaten; Widmark focusing an elephant gun on her head—I got up, pulled down my jeans, spread myself before the dressing mirror and scrutinized the organization of bits locked there. It didn't look anything like the face of a monkey. More madness. Unless he meant the kind of red-lipped, know-nothing monkey moms make out of socks. You could think of it that way. Of course, once I'd thought of it that way, I couldn't think of it any other. It had the nasty insistence of a radio jingle you can't get out of your head. Like, "Eat Eskimo Pie. Eat Eskimo Pie."

The Phantom Limb

"Something must be the matter with a patient who consults a physician when in fact nothing is the matter."
—K. White
"Health Care Arrangements in the United States"

This is a story that could only have taken place where it did, in the town where I grew up, Carthage, Illinois, just north of Mark Twain's Hannibal, right near the modern Mississippi. For complex reasons, Carthage has become *the* place where what is present and what is not is most gravely questioned.

This story concerns my mother and her peculiar distress, my father, my sister Tia, and myself, Dwayne. One morning I was home alone watching the *Dialing for Dollars* movie starring Joseph Cotten (how he falls in love, is somebody's boob, protests convincingly, meets the suggestive alien in a taxi and leaves us all in doubt about whether Life is Fair). I expected my mother home for lunch. It was her morning routine to meet the girls for one of her usuals at the Tavern, then return home to change the channel, sit in the mom's chair, and eat the lunch I'd prepared.

Well, she came home as I anticipated, but something was wrong. Where was that sprite in her stepping that

Smirnoffs gave her? She rather scraped by me; she moved as does a grasshopper pinned by a wiper blade. Far beneath the weather, I thought. What's more, she didn't even stop to change the channel in order to watch the Perry Mason case (that day: "The Body of the Missing Person"). At first, I was hurt, because I took Mom's indifference to my zeal (over what fantastic sinks of money were accruing on Dialing for Dough) as an expression of affection.

"Are you OK, Mom?" I asked.

"Oh, Butch," she said in her gruff loving way, "I do feel a mite peculiar." Then she straightened the hem of her plaid skirt.

Not much later I noticed Mom rubbing her left arm up and down, and pinching it as if it were a rolled roast. Jesus! I concluded. She's having a heart attack! And there's so much I haven't told her. You know how it is between a boy and his mom, how the essence of their affection seems forever deferred.

So I said to her, "Mom, what's the matter? What's wrong with your arm?"

She looked at me with some kind of shock, like no son could be either that stupid or that cruel.

"Even though I've lost this arm," she explained, "every once in a while I'll feel it twitching out there. Or it will ache like I'd been lifting babies or sacks of flour or hauling carp up from the river."

Lost her arm? Had my mother lost her arm?

"But Mom. You still have your arm."

"Don't be an idiot, Son. I remember it as well as you

do. A radial arm saw, a machete, the whirring blades of the reaper, the unsuspected blood, the empty veins green in the sun."

"Do you mean you can't see it now, there on your chair?"

"Of course not."

"But you can see your other, your right arm?"

"Why sure."

This scared me. I wanted her quickly to confess that her arm hung at her side as arms do for the rest of us. So I grabbed a mirror off our wall and confronted her with it.

"See there, Mom. You have got your arm."

I peeked around the side of the mirror to see her expression, the surprise and relief. Instead, her face contorted with a scowl of disgust as if she'd been shown that her organs clung to the wrong side, her intestines drooping like an uncinched belt, her heart banging away raw as a skinned rodent. Shocked, I crooked my head around to have a look, but of course I saw only my own face, my hispid nostrils plummeting like sinkholes into meat.

"Oh, Sonny," she cried, "Don't be so mean. I can't bear it."

* * *

Later, Dad and Sister came home from shopping. They were laughing and chattering, big sacks full of mall prizes in their arms. But they caught themselves and came stock-still in the middle of the room when they saw me in my Mr. Somber routine and Mom a bag of ash in her chair.

Sister Tia tried to take control. "What's the matter with Mom, Dwayne?"

"She says her phantom limb is bothering her."

"And what phantom limb would that be, Son?" asked Dad.

"She claims to have lost her left arm in an encounter with a blade of some sort and, moreover, to have seen it displayed in the sun."

Dad and Tia exchanged knowing looks, nodding gravely.

"I think Mom is feeling a sort of social inadequacy," suggested Tia. "She is finding it difficult to fulfill her obligations to the community. It is the old story of stress."

"Something we've been seeing a lot of," said Dad, smiling with a silly confidence.

"Yes indeed. And this is Mom's way of taking some time off. She will play the role of one of the sick until she is ready to resume her responsibilities."

"In short," I said, "she has the Malady."

The three of us then lifted her like Old King Cole from his throne and transported her to bed. And there she stayed for the next several weeks, suffering not only from pain in not-her-arm, but from apathy, fatigue, and from the most uncharacteristic indifference to her own opinions. Not unfamiliar states for you and me, perhaps, but for a spirit as robust as Mom's, painfully inappropriate.

It was the beginning of a very difficult period for us. Of course, I stayed home, at her bedside, flipping through the television channels, hoping for her old excitement about programs to return, but the spark, the isolate flicker, the originary throb in her was gone. Gone for *Hawaii Five-O*, gone for *The Untouchables*, gone even for the magic, the surreal chemistry of *Combat*. It was not a lot easier for Tia and Dad. Sure, they continued to attend the mall, but they returned early, their ample shopping bags containing only a minimum purchase. Still, they would show Mom, for example, a silken blouse that Dad had picked out for Sister, which draped her front and back in a way that made Dad gape. But we looked in vain for that old congratulation which Mom used to lavish on their choices. They received only a tepid "That's nice" in its place.

Finally, one day toward spring, we drove her to Chicago to see a specialist, knowing in our hearts how futile such an effort was, knowing that there were no specialists in the Malady. But Mother encouraged us anyway, confident that the enormous consultation fee would make us cheerful for a while. I can still see her in the back of the car passing spoons and other objects through her arm. Dad was amused and asked her to exhibit her knack to our fellow motorists. I was silent. Sister kept her hands on the wheel, her eye on the road.

* * *

"Did you bring the specimen?" Dr. Allegro did not waste time.

Dad removed a small white bracelet box from his pocket in which was a plastic sandwich bag in which was Mom's specimen.

"Did I make that?" asked Mom.

"Yes, Dear."

"I don't remember."

It was a color we didn't associate with Mother.

"Good. Thank you. I'll be right back. A nurse will be in to take other samples."

"What are you going to do with that, Dr. Allegro?" asked Sister.

"I'm going to put it in the centrifuge, then I'm going to look at it under the microscope, then I'm going to introduce it to certain chemicals."

"Can we watch?"

"Of course, if you'd like."

Unfortunately, as we had feared, when Dr. Allegro had coerced all the information he could from Mom's multiform excesses, he had little to offer us.

"She is physiologically well," he said, "relatively speaking. That is, nothing is wrong with her that isn't wrong with many another hardy Illinoisian. Specifically, my findings point toward a condition that has attacked your mother in a diffuse, generalized fashion, to which insult she has responded by nonspecific symptoms indicating organic and psychoemotional distress. She complains of pain in her dorsolumbar region, lack of appetite, asthenia, and fatigue. My tests indicate that she suffers from nonspecific anemia and from intestinal parasitosis (amoebic). Needless to say, none of this is in itself fatal and none of it explains the gravity of your mother's condition. Her hematocrit level and our lung scrapings lead me to suspect that she is presently experiencing what I would describe as a generalized, systemic meditation on disease. In short, there is no way for me to know, but your mother may have the Malady.

"Inclusion of the Malady in a patient's medical history tips the balance towards death."

* * *

It is part of the virtue of life in the midwest that when the technology and sophistication of the modern world fails, when what it can deduce from life-stuff centrifuged to a fine essence, read over with a laser scan, and absolutely rendered by digital computers is inadequate, there are always the grosser traditions of our heart-of-the-country ways to fall back on. Long before the recent apotheosis of high-tech reckoning, we had our own, perhaps savage, science thanks to which we had thrived for centuries. So, when luxurious death seduced our parents' parents, they didn't drive to smart-guy "experts" in Chicago. Rather, they called upon the lonely figure of the Mayor. In the past, it was he who conferred with the families of those stricken with the Malady. It was his soothsaying that held the promise of repair, recovery, and reconciliation with social duty. It was such an aboriginal understanding that led my mother, at an otherwise fatal degree of her illness, to lift herself on her one elbow and declare, "Fetch Mayor Huedepohl. He'll know what to do."

What do you imagine are the responsibilities of the mayor of a place like Carthage? Keep the cops away from the taverns on Saturday night. Keep the drinking water safely chlorinated. Collect the hundred-dollar salary at the end of each month. Be fat and functional. Well, just such a mayor was our Mayor Huedepohl. He had been held as no-account as long as I could remember, but he had been mayor longer than that. And at some obscure point in the past he must have been acquainted with the skills my mother's instructions assumed. For when he came to our house, there was no question of his purpose. He knew what to do.

Dad, Sister, and I sat with him in chairs at the side of my mother's bed. First—and this was the gesture with which he set our admiration—he took from his pocket a nicely carved and lapis-inlaid soapstone case in which wriggled a dozen fat leeches, curling like ravenous pinkies. Without a word he extracted two and attached them one each to mother's earlobes, where they dangled brutally.

"There," he said, "that should buy some time." Then he turned to us. "You were most wrong to wait so long. Your mother is at the edge and we'll be lucky to bring her back."

My father began whimpering at this point and the Mayor directed him to leave the room. Then, with just Tia and myself left to aid him, he asked, "Has your mother been frightened by anything recently? Has she had some terrifying experience?"

We didn't know how to respond.

"Let me explain. Often the Malady is incurred at a vulnerable moment at which an Aire (an evil spirit) is able to transport Virtu from the body. At a moment of intense fright, when the mouth and eyes are gaping open, your mother might have been thus vulnerable. So, do you recall any such incidents?"

After about twenty minutes of talk we concluded that there were the following possibilities for experience of fright:

- She had been startled by the bark of the neighbor's dog, Doberman.
- She had dreamed again of the traveling salesman with the briefcase full of spiders.
- A drunk had breathed on her.
- She had inadvertently seen my father's genitalia.
- It had occurred to her that she didn't understand how blood worked and that therefore it shouldn't.

I argued persuasively that of course it was the fright of seeing my father's penis that had given her such a shock, at which point Dad, who had been listening at the door, rushed in and claimed that our mother hadn't seen his concoction in, lo!, these last five years, and that it was no shabby article to look upon even if she had. The Mayor instructed my erring father to shut the door behind him.

My sister felt it was the breath of a drunk that had given my mother her evil turn, because the breath of a drunk is vaporous like a swamp and full of disease. However, through the Mayor's expert negotiations we were able to conclude that it was certainly some frightful wrong-thinking about the presumed functioning of organs that had precipitated her present situation.

He therefore left us with the following prescription: "Keep the worms applied to her ears and should they get too fat with blood replace them with two of their pale cousins. Then sing of them: 'THEY EAT US! They are not our brothers. They are worms, wild beasts.' In the meantime, bring a large round hollow gourd or an old red tea kettle into the room. Into these you are to repeat, 'Come back, Mom, come back, sweet one.' The greater the distance that separates her vital essence from her body, the more often will you need to call her name into the containers. And you should from time to time reassure her with words to this effect, 'It's okay, Mom, your lungs remember how to breathe. Your kidneys understand their responsibilities.' The effect of these remedies, all chanted simultaneously, should be a lot like that of children singing a round. It should also be quite potent."

We thanked Mayor Huedepohl greedily and Tia promised to wear for him the silken-blouse-at-which-men-gape as a little token. This made Dad angry, so before he committed another childish excess we took the Mayor to the door. Just before he left, he turned to us and asked, his face betraying for the first time the dangerous perplexity of my mother's condition, "When did your mother lose her arm?"

* * *

Most people deny that there is anything metaphysical about the midwest. And it is true that the crust of the normal is more than usually thick here. But a distress like my mother's can create a sort of crevice in that crust through which we may peep in order to see forgotten things, like the fact that men are animals and animals are gods. Well, we were pushed to this extreme of perception and beyond in caring for our mother. For we applied the Mayor's remedies diligently, creatively, but they made no change in her condition. She continued to lay in bed, a sluggard to all curative suggestion, her tender absent arm sleeping among pillows.

The ultimate, desperate degree of her treatment was at last described by the Mayor. We were to perform at her bedside, for her benefit, the awesome Dance of the Countless Grievances (known elsewhere—in Decatur, Joliet, and the Quad Cities—as the Dance of Charitable Ardor or of the Legitimate Motive), severely though such a dance was sure to tax those of the family still in health. The purpose of the risk was of course to shock Mom back to some sense of responsibility to the basic styles of her people.

The situation was this. My mother slept in her bed, in her peculiar and changeable coma, her absent arm glowing softly like a child's night light. Then through the bedroom door came my sister, draped in gauzy stuff, a basket of carnations at her belly into which she dipped her fingers tenderly. On her face was a small, gently carved mask, the Novia, from the lurching ears of which hung pink glass earrings. Well, she pranced around

Mom's bed tossing the flowers and prating nonsense like something that would have gotten Botticelli worked up. Finally, from the bottom of the basket she pulled a long, thick rawhide strap, hinged and with a leather knot at its end. Then in the door came I, similarly masked, the Novio, a mustache smartly adorning my upper lip, a neatly carved, red-tipped cigarette poking just-so from the corner of my mouth. (To tell the truth, I didn't know what I was supposed to do, but there must have been some magic in all this, because just my entrance caused Mother to go rigid, as if she'd gotten a high-volt shock of jolt therapy.)

For my part, I sort of tottered in Tia's direction, feeling as awkward as a marionette, and performed a courtly tap dance, arms akimbo, the purpose of which was plainly to encourage her to some form of excess. She responded with required coyness, holding the leather truncheon before her mask-lips as if it were a dainty fan or the thighbone of a pig. But I was a persistent admirer and at last offered the object of my affection my hand in matrimony to which idea she signaled her pleasure by reaching beneath my pantaloons and retrieving a leather strap identical to hers. Then, while tapping the lips of our masks together happily, we performed a bit of horse-play and vulgar humor in which local scandals and peoples' weaknesses were referred to.

Then in stormed our father. He wore a mask unlike ours. It was an angry blue-green with killing eyes, devil's horns, bat's ears and in his awful eating mouth the body of a blue snake that curled about his face, the blunt head of the snake eventually becoming his nose. (The snake-snout was a conventionalized allusion to one of our Carthage Pork Days activities, during which certain men would gather around a water trough and bob for the reluctant and fleeting bodies of frogs and serpents. He who first seized with his teeth and swallowed one of the creatures was greeted with a great hullabaloo and offered gifts which he could accept or reject as it pleased him.) Into our happiness our father waded, disrupting our dance and really frightening us, getting us out of his way. When he felt he had control, he produced a knife and made as if to strike the sleeping figure of our mother. But at that moment—even though I felt my role was simply to watch as the knife found my mother's heart—Tia brought the sturdy knot of her leather cord down on Dad's head, her mask reflecting a kind of cruelty and glee I'm certain she really felt. For I felt it and quickly joined in. And soon we were beating out some sort of primitive rhumba on his pater noggin. Bossa Nova!

Dad was a good sport about it all—"Hey, kids! Easy does it!"—but he kept his complaints at a whisper, not wanting to jeopardize this cure. "Whoa, honey! That one smarted!" But it soon became plain—as the mask stove in, the snake's would-be ferocity chipped, and the blows began to arrive on Dad-head itself— that this was the happiest our family had ever been. Finally, Dad announced that there would be "an award for agrarian reform, based on the need of previously landless peasants" at which point Sister reared back and delivered a ground zero blow that crushed our father's mask, which held the leather knot like a sunken cannon ball and inspired a gush of stuff, as if we'd just burst a bladder full of ox blood. Dad fell on the floor and was real quiet like.

I didn't know what to make of most of this. It was Tia who seemed in the know. Apparently, we weren't done. She pushed me back on the bed, right next to Mom, and with one snatch tore away the crotch of my trousers. Much to my surprise, my own member stood like a sapling (Was it wooden too? Was it a sort of mask?) painted in alternating red and blue vertical stripes and with a festive green bow around its head. Then she was on me and all I remember besides a distant and impersonal bliss was the relentless knocking together of our masked faces which rattled my head like a gourd full of pinto beans.

It was then that the magic of our dance had its effect. Shocking, from one side, two strong arms wrapped us and the certain and rigorous sound of our mother's voice boomed:

"NOW JUST WHAT IN THE HELL DO YOU KIDS THINK YOU'RE DOING?"

"Mom," we said, "You've come back to us!"

"Of course I've come back, for goodness' sake. What does that mean? And where is your father? He'd better not see you like this or you'll catch it."

We pulled Dad up from the floor, all of us weeping and trembling, and he said faintly, "Honey? Is that you?"

"Sure it's me, you idiot. Butch, go out to the garage and get some of those rags to sop up this mess on his head."

"Yes, Mom!"

And thus it was that the spirit, the essential fire of our mother was called back and her sense of purpose restored.

A Disciplined Life

1. I am taken to the penitentiary

On that night, we had been in mysterious America for only a few months. I, Daniel Campabruno, and my most satisfactory wife, beautiful Michelle, we slept in a bed big enough for the two of us (although out of old habit and a desire that was never far off, we lay as close as lips). In the next room was the loving flesh of our flesh, our little girl, Beatrice, "Trisha" to her American friends.

We had been forced to leave our fine home in Naples because all of Italy was at that time under the spell of the great ass in jackboots. He would not tolerate a man like myself, a poet and philosopher in the old style, and so my family and I, seeing no other alternative, left discreetly, bound for New York. Oh, certainly, my wife cried at leaving the land of bright sun, *O paese d' 'o sole*. But our expectations of this great, grey land—to which our countrymen had been traveling for decades—were also bright.

Imagine, then, our disappointment when we found that New York was already full of many people of many countries living close and poor in New York's smallest,

darkest corners. We were no worse off in Naples. For here sheer numbers would keep a man from rising to distinction. Fortunately, my breathtaking 'Cella, with her great understanding, said that while we still had the money we should take one of the dark American trains and go to a place where the people were fewer and the opportunities greater. So we traveled, racketing along the miraculous rails, to Chicago, and then south to the welcome town of Mallet, Illinois. We were joyed at the prospects for happiness.

But I discovered before long, long before we discovered our happiness, what a very sensitive, particular and disciplined people the Illinois are. For in just a matter of weeks, without ever realizing it, I myself, the one upon whom my family depended, had outraged the laws of that state in any number of ways. I had proceeded illegally, if naively. I had in dismaying ignorance violated principles (understood by everyone but myself) of propriety, decorum, decency. I had trespassed, caused material loss, breach of faith, personal trauma and—in cases that haunt and amaze me even now—bodily pain. My memories of those days are the memories of a man whose head has been wrapped in a fog as tight as the bandings on a lunatic, who pleads with those furious citizens around him, "Forgive me. Explain this to me."

It was therefore of little surprise when on a hot, damp July evening, as my family slept, there came a man, representative of the state, knocking at the door to the house which homed our much subdued hopes. I, of course, was the one to get up, remove myself miserably from my darling's closeness, and answer the polite but insistent caller. It was the purposeful Anderson Smyth, officer of corrections for the State Penitentiary at Halbert.

I want to say to my readers, especially my American readers, that I have nothing against corrections or the officers thereof. But I would suggest that they (the corrections, the adjustments) be made *before* a well-meaning, misfortuned man like myself is allowed to join the life in progress and make a muck of things. There can be better screening and perhaps a brief program for us on arrival.

But, to my story. Officer Smyth stood before me and said, as I expected, "It is time for you to come with me." I knew what he meant, but you will understand if I say I was afraid. Again, I want you to realize that I hold nothing against Officer Smyth and in fact regard Anderson (as he eventually encouraged me to call him) as a close and dear friend. He is tall, straight, fair of feature and more just than any other man I have ever known.

I turned in order to put together a few belongings, but was instantly stopped by Anderson who explained that all of my needs would now be met by the state. I looked at him then in what I can tell you was nothing other than panic and said, "But of course my family—my wife, my little Beatrice—they may come with me?"

"Mr. Campabruno," he answered, "Your family may not join you, but they may follow if they choose. Many of the families of our residents do choose to follow. In order to be close. It is their right. They may even ride with us if they like. It is, to tell you the truth, a long drive to Halbert and I am not forbidden."

Here was the hope offered us that our life was not wholly ruined. I ran to my wife and asked her to dress. She understood what was happening. I next went to the room of my little Trisha, who slept the deep unencumbered sleep of a child. I shook her gently and she lifted herself, scraping her tiny fists against her eyes and looking dimly around.

The drive from Mallet to Halbert was melancholy. 'Cella sat quietly and only rarely cried into a handkerchief. But Trisha, being but four and understanding nothing, wanted to know where we were going. Why? Why was Mama crying? And what was it I had done that was bad? She sat in my lap the whole way—already missing me—her arms wrapped about my neck. Anderson turned to us occasionally from his front seat and—looking as if from a great distance, his face betraying none of the gusty emotions I can but imagine he felt—passed into our area of the car small objects that were of great use to us. Parcels of gum, paper, a cigarette for myself. Beyond him the car's headlamps intruded with a kind of misery on the darkness through which ran U.S. route 51.

When at last we arrived at Halbert, had parked our automobile and walked across the grounds, we were taken past a set of doors through which we peered down a long corridor of cells. It was like what I had always imagined Father Dominic meant by *infinitus*. One after another of something without ever stopping.

In the middle of the corridor hung electric lamps. In my gloom they looked to me like the suicides of sacred, brilliant bodies, hung by their radiant skulls. And there were numberless brackets at the ceiling, beautifully ornamental. I was ashamed to think that when this building was first constructed, lovely wrought angels reclined along their tops. But the fury of the attendants at Halbert had led them to remove the little angels, as if to say, "Because of what we use this building for, because of what those who must come here have done, there may be no angels."

When we came to the end of the corridor, two somber gentlemen waited to question me. Anderson Smyth was still at my side, his arm now for the first time lightly gripping my elbow. My wife and little one, awed, stood back a step. An older man spoke to me. "Your name?" I was about to reply when Anderson interrupted. "This is Daniel Campabruno, convicted alien."

Perhaps there had been an unnatural pause before my own answer. I would learn the rhythm of this place.

"And he is to be held . . ."

"In maximum security."

The old man looked up at me. "You'll be with us for twenty years, then, Mr. Campabruno?"

I was cast down by this fact. "The judge mentioned something which I believe I understood. If I am good, if I learn how to conduct myself among Americans, I may be put on pay roll?"

"Parole."

"Yes."

"If you are very good, Mr. Campabruno."

Suddenly the younger man who had been sitting took me by the arm and led me quickly to a large solid door which led to an even deeper recess of the prison. I was surprised. I had no time for goodbyes or last kisses with my little, lost ones. I had just the time to turn as I went through the door to see the wide, bright, uncertain eyes of my 'Cella, my Trisha, and the broad, firm, surrounding arms of Anderson Smyth.

2. I am shown my cell

Like a man who can put off the pain of anything (the certain death of parents, the suffering of one's own children, the approach of unpleasant appointments) until the very moment itself, until he is actually having to take the hand of the dying father and press the emaciated fingers to his lips, it was not until I was led down those gray, unfamiliar corridors, past the sad, sleeping forms of my fellow convicted, that I realized how awful this was. I was to be separated from my family, made indifferent to their fates, closed in a building as snug as a grave. I began to bend at the knees and would have fallen were it not for the official at my side.

But when at last we reached my own cell, and the heavy door was swung back, I was presented with a vision as contradictory and baffling as any knot of philosophy. There in an imperturbably bright light was no European gaol, but a home, a little home, like neither

I nor any of my ancestors had ever known. There were side tables and a beautiful scrolled wicker chair, a bed with a quilt cover, pictures on the walls, flowers in vases, even a good Catholic corner with a cross clean as Volterran alabaster. Best of all, I was to be allowed a guitar on which I could amuse myself—during appropriate hours— playing the Neapolitan songs of my country, people, youth. In a strange ecstasy, cousin to suicidal gloom, I leaped through the entrance, landed on two feet, desired to embrace or devour this room, realized how wild the turn in my emotions must look to my attendant and, so, returned to him. But his face, all I can say is that I may have been delirious. When I looked to him his face did not seem, but actually swam with mixing, blackening clouds. It was like the levels of clouds during thundering Illinois storms. I wanted to ask about my wife and child, wanted to ask when I could see them, to ask about the regimen plotted for me, but how could anyone question this amazing being?

He stood for a moment with folded arms before me, his face swirling, and then slammed closed my cell door.

* * *

It was a week before I was scheduled for an interview with my wife and daughter. How I longed to hold them over the table which now separated our fortunes. How I longed to breach all regulations, lean across that barrier and hug my little baby. You can imagine my disappointment, then, when none other than Anderson Smyth waited for me. Where could they be, my loved ones?

"Mr. Smyth," I said, sitting myself in a sturdy wooden chair, "I understood that this was to be time when I could visit with my family."

Smyth was always very patient with me. He took out a cigarette and lit it. He looked at me with great clarity. "Perhaps," he said, "at another time that will be possible."

"I hope you can at least tell me if they are well."

He looked at me with blame and contempt, a look I'd never known in my own country. "Oh, they're well enough, no thanks to yourself."

What could he mean by this? The tremendous anger, compulsiveness of my race (what may, perhaps, now that I consider it, have been responsible for my predicament to begin with) began to roar in me. I nearly stood up. "What do you mean?" I demanded.

"Oh," he said, puffing, "It's just that it was stupid of you to bring your family here when they had no money and no place to stay. What arrangements had you made? You had your own little cell (and a comfortable one at that), but you left your family standing in the hall, virtually abandoned."

Then, of course, the memory of my joy in my room returned, that space of beauty and solitude which had returned me to the ancient consolations of philosophy and art which were my birthright. The keen blade of guilt punctured my tentative sack of rage. Was Smyth not suggesting that I preferred the solitary pleasures of prison to life with my own family?

I then asked more moderately, "So, what has become of them? Do they hate me very much?"

Smyth smiled for the first time and I saw his tapered teeth. "In their need, I offered them a spare room in my own home. They are safe and well there. How they feel about you, you will have to ask."

I stood up, prepared to return to my cell, confident that this competent American could care for my loved ones. "Thank you, Mr. Anderson Smyth."

3. I am given work; I try something desperate

Within the first few days of my long, vivid stay at Halbert I was given work. I was taken to an enormous room, a sort of field within a vault. There, I saw row after row of tables, one set hard upon the other, receding, removed into such an impossible distance that I could not imagine that what I saw was real. There were other things I could not imagine. In the world, were there enough people to sit at so many plates? And surely there were not so many crimes, there could not be enough viciousness. How had so many men been undone? But, on the other hand, it had not been difficult for authorities to find me. So, if the others were like me, they had all stepped forward, their guilt like something rancid on their breath.

Just imagine if my great countryman, Dante, lingering in Paradise, had seen this vision. Wouldn't he have said, "Like the brilliant hammered gold plates set on the great tables at the feast of a king, the bright souls of the saved arranged themselves before me"? But that, of course, was what was so strange and contradictory. We

accused, accursed. But in this mysterious America, this place of odd forgivenesses and generosities, even those of us in prison were provided with an incongruous beauty.

However, all was not bliss for me. One day I sat in a circle at my job, with my co-convicted, peeling mountains of potatoes. In our group, old Tony—a talented blasphemer—told us his rumors, jokes and nonsense. Tony was allowed to keep a ground hog, Edgar, who hunched on his shoulder and gobbled potato peels. The animal seemed to mark Tony's special role. Most of what he said was only amusing, but one day he spoke of Anderson Smyth and in a way that drove me to great recklessness.

"I understand," he said, "that Officer Smyth has got himself a new woman." Fleshy potato lay heaped at his feet like shavings from the Madonna's thigh. "And you boys all know about Smyth, don't you. You know how he pleasures himself. They say that he's got this piece of meat that's like the devil's own. They say that he used to rub it every day with a billy club and that now the darned thing is so dark, so thick, so like lead that that billy might as well been its mama. Well, you know Smyth's house is close to a mile away. Still, the fellas on the west wing swear that every night from eleven to witchin' time they can hear the howls, rapture, agony of this new gal bein' topped off. If she had an entrance wide as her rib cage, it would be tight for Smyth."

I dropped the potato I held and left. I insisted to a guard that I be allowed to speak with the Warden. It was not allowed. I demanded an interview with my wife. Not tolerated. With Smyth. Impossible.

It was then that I decided that I must escape, break out of the state penitentiary at Halbert.

* * *

First, of course, I stole a spoon. To this simple spoon I applied the undeniable whetstone of patience and bloodthirst, my great will to revenge. For week upon week I drew it affectionately against my concrete floor, my bit of hone, that which was to put a point on my rage. Were these Americans so poorly researched? Didn't they know with what quality they mixed? Did they know nothing of the bloody history of my people? Of Lorenzo? Of forgiveless Cosimo? Of Condottiere Sigismundo, who would kill his own kin when the thirst was in him?

When at last my spoon was sufficient, I went at a crumbling pocket of mortar and brick which when I was through would leave me a clean, pure drop to the prison courtyard. From there, I hoped that strength, guile, calm, and determination would get me beyond the prison outposts and fences. From there I was nothing more than loping distance from the white clapboard home of Anderson Smyth. Of course, along the way into my hands would fall—as what is necessary comes to the inspired, to the blessed, to the mad—instruments appropriate to my purpose: chains, blades, explosives, the raging pincers of my ancestry.

What kept me keen to my purpose over those many weeks as I dug, scraped, ignored the bone peeking through at my fingertips, were the visions (God-sent, certain as glory) of the horrors perpetrated on my little ones. As if I were nothing more than an ear and an eye, perched on a branch outside Anderson Smyth's rooms, I endured and was spurred on by the moans and suffering of my sweet Michelle. And then occasionally to the window, a ghost, an emaciated ghoul, came my Trisha, looking for her papa.

* * *

I am no longer proud of the tenacity which allowed me, even after my spoon had been worn down to a bit of steel too small to be held, to claw my way through brick. You see, only a person who was sick, who was touched with the disease of a certain foreign mentality, could have succeeded in such a feat. Nor am I pleased with the memory of leaping a fence twice my height, or maiming guard dogs any number of times more strong and cunning, but not half as devilish, as myself. How I tore at them, how I made them regret their proud responsibilities.

But what was it for? Dear Creator, for what purpose did I strive? I had been placed in prison and I resented it. I then went about to kill the man who had placed me in prison ... and with that murderous intention I reaffirmed just why I had been put in jail. But, you say, if Smyth had stolen my loved ones, my family, then I had just cause. Judge, now, from my experience if I had just cause.

I crept toward Smyth's home. No brute ever crept lower, kept more maliciously to the covering ground. Up to a window I went. I expected to see Smyth naked, covered with a rich mat of hair, rending my darling and holding at arm's length, a strangling hand at her throat, my little Beatrice. But this is what I saw in fact: 'Cella sat in a large, comfortable chair, buried in its generosity of cushions, a well-adjusted reading lamp above her, and a copy of the American magazine LIFE in her lap. On the other side of the room was Trisha (hardly emaciated, a solid five pounds happier) in the lap of Anderson Smyth. On her head was a baseball cap; on the RCA radio were the New York Yankees playing the Chicago White Sox; on Smyth's lips were patient explanations of the rules of the great American game.

4. Discipline

Thus the tale of my old life—how I had failed myself, my family, my adopted country. But this is also—thankfully—the story of the beginning of my new life. I returned myself to the state penitentiary at Halbert, submitted myself to the amazed guards. I realized that my mad act would add to my tenure, but I knew also that I was still far from ready to leave. I knew that I needed much more time, that I was not yet adequate to join the life in progress in this strange, beautiful country.

About five patient, suffering years into my term, Michelle applied for divorce and the Church, awed by my conduct, readily decreed in her favor. Of course, I was only too glad to agree, knowing what improvements

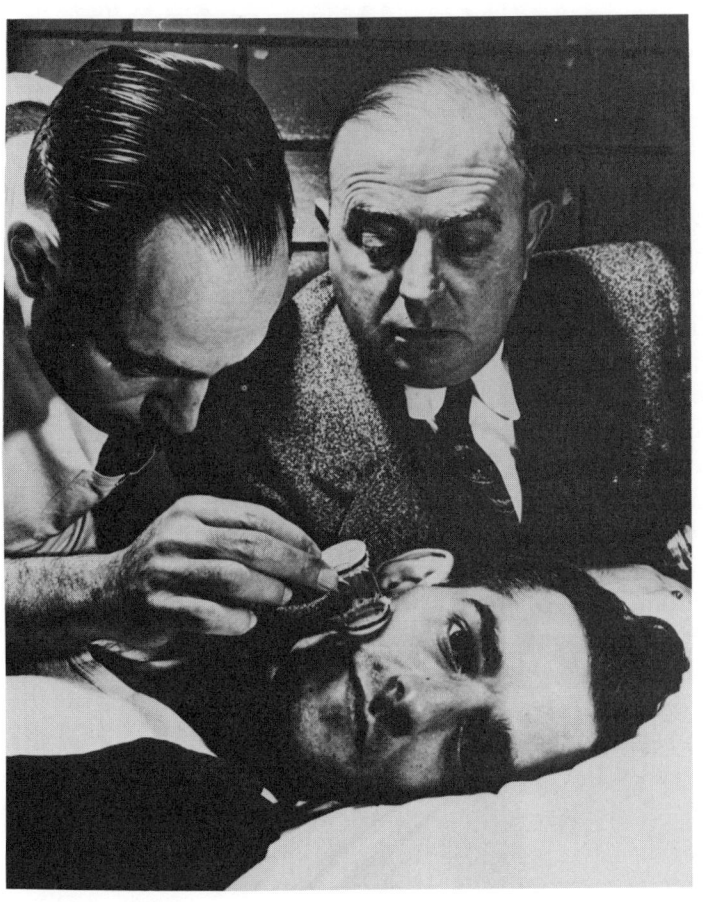

such an arrangement would bring to my family. Two years later Michelle and Anderson Smyth married and they now live with Beatrice and two children of their own in Kansas City, Missouri, where Anderson is a prosperous grocer.

For myself, I have spent these many years learning. Like the monks of my old country, like Bruno and the saints, I have submitted myself to the lifelong effort of discipline. No longer do I live in the vain, embellished cell to which I was first introduced and which was so appropriate to that old life. In my present cell the walls are bare and there is no deluding guitar.

In pursuit of this great discipline, this docility I seek, I volunteer myself for the Warden's most arduous projects. Just this morning I reported to the prison hospital to aid in an important experiment. I lay on a table. A scientist and even the Warden himself bent above me. To my face they brought a small vial covered with a light cloth at each end. In the vial was an avid mosquito. The vial was placed on my face. The bite of the creature was painful and sweet, but I gave no indication that the little beast had hurt me. I am told that the Warden was very pleased.

More Crimes Against the People of Illinois

"Girls will be girls, but they should be restrained."
—Lucy Page Gaston,
Anti-cigarette crusader

That's how it is with the past. Insinuator. Troublemaker. I was in a dusty, peevish mood, loading boxes with old books, when two photographs slipped from between the shrouded pages of a law primer, a book I couldn't remember setting fingers to in fifteen years, not since that dusky time when I studied the law in Chicago. But, to tell the truth, I couldn't remember even then willingly holding the pictures—subtle, candid portraits—as I was suddenly again made to hold them. It wasn't that I didn't know these "subjects," sad, maybe even tragic, but nonetheless preposterous people that they were. Here was Jeannette, obtruding, as you can see, in an otherwise seamless vista of typists, women making a record of the customer's order; on her face is a look of impossible longing. And here Franklin, cordial, delirious, perhaps criminal, not daring to face the camera's dark eye.

Now memory, like a bubble of gas, will of course rise lethally to the surface. And so it is that I see myself, a much younger man, eighteen, moving north in the car of my Uncle Hiram, headed for the great city of doubt, Chicago.

I grew up in the central Illinois town of Dun, the town of "Astonishing Fortune," I think it should be called. For I remember little more of my youth than the astonished expressions on the faces of the people of Dun, the queerest mixture of Irish Catholic, Italian, and German immigrants, who found that in the drab soil of their lives-to-that-point had blossomed unpredictably the most amazing flower of any American genus, prosperity. Dun was, for no reason its people could fathom other than God's depthless will, an important center for shipping corn, beans, wheat, and livestock on the Alton-Chicago line. Wagons of grain as infinite and profound as time, stone, or grief rolled into Dun. There were days when wagons, trucks and tractors stretched on every highway, in every direction, to the horizon. The summer heat, striking off the roads, and the plunging late afternoon sun gave to this scene a shifting, contrived look.

Of course, everybody in Dun got "fat": real estate people, bankers, merchants, board of trade folk, railroad owners and stockholders. Thus the utter surprise, the utter, smiling, splendid surprise of everybody's wealth feeding everybody else's wealth. The mild, euphoric sound of the word *America* was never more than a breath away from their startled lips. And then the houses went up: Italianate, Second Empire, Neoclassical, a Queen Anne mansion. Never a better time to see people in love with their lives. America was a dream.

That is, there was something unreal about it. Especially for a youngster growing up smothered by the success of his parents and their generation. What resistance was there against which to test my own strength? What contradiction to my own will? I was—I tell you the truth although you may not admire it— made a little sick by my parent's happiness. There was something angry about my blood, and I was impatient with the sight of Dun's massive satisfaction.

Break it, I said. Hurt it.

But what can an eighteen-year-old do to fracture the great thighbone of contentment? The worst I could do was confound all the sensible supposing of my family, leave what seemed well and good enough for anybody, and accept the ride offered by my loose-to-rattling Uncle Hiram. Thereby, at least, I caused a vague unease in the heart of the bone, in the marrow of my parents' life, which would—like some sulking cancer—not declare itself for years.

That is how I explain the motives that moved me to abandon a life of the most predictable happiness. But what do any of us know of motives? I have no desire to appear noble, I have no fear of seeming materialistic. Let us say, then, that I left my hometown of Dun not because its prosperity was petty, but because it was *petit*, too small a thing for me. Let us say that my Uncle Hiram could offer me access to a world in which people of real wealth and real power lived. For if those others—

those men who came and went on State Street—could have it, why couldn't I?

What my uncle Hiram proposed to me was a clerical job in dark Chicago with the Sears and Roebuck Company, whose multiform growth and division under the famous Mr. Julius Rosenwald was amazing to all who beheld it. For anyone with skills in figures or letters, explained Uncle Hiram, there was a job in Chicago. Of course, beginning pay for a young man such as myself— without a family to support, just getting started in the world—was only fifteen dollars per week. But if I showed talent and diligence, I would be noted and I would receive promotion. I could count on it. The world is not unfair, young man!

Ah, but memory is a candid, a plainspoken coward. It gets the facts out, but it offers to do nothing about them. So, yes, I made my fortune in Chicago. My riches could now bust the back of every man, woman, and child in Dun. And those whose backs it couldn't break, it could sicken. But also in Chicago, on the way to my fortune, I met Franklin and Jeannette, in particular Jeannette. But if not Jeannette, then some other one else. For all women are like her. All women cloak, allow to abide in their heart of hearts, embloused, as it were, such a spirit as Jeannette's.

* * *

"Are you busy for dinner tonight? Can you come to my house?"

Was it just good fortune to be given a desk beside such

a generous man? Or did it make a difference where I sat? Was every male in the letter room determined to be kind to solitary young men? Would any of them have asked me home? (Especially me, a person on whom the appearance of youth, innocence, harmlessness meant absolutely nothing.) Or was it just good, kind, feckless Franklin?

Franklin X. was like one of those placid, kindly sea mammals; he was a sort of dextrous dolphin. How else to describe this looming, affectionate, essentially thoughtless blimp of flesh. If you had only once heard the sighing of his lovemaking, like the sweet piping song of a whale, you would take no other description seriously.

"And you can meet my friend," he said. "Jeannette. She works here too, you know. She'll be glad to meet you."

Yes, Jeannette too worked with Sears, making a record of the customer's order. But she was not one of those dull creatures insensitive to the brutality of working with lists of numbers, the ransom of others' will to possess, infinite as grains of sand. She resented the tedium of her job, both for herself and for her fellow workers. But she was also one of those who could make herself forgetful of her irksome duty and hang instead at a superior, hazier level. Discorporated. Thinking her own thoughts. Seeing unbelievable things. Would anyone disagree if I said this was the level of the poem?

At times she became so involved in her own visions that the office became a strange, pulsing, and unpredictable sea of cabinets, files, and miraculous corridors.

Women were multiplied endlessly up one aisle and another, their hair, shining and clean, piled on their heads; their white blouses glistening. If at such times she was struck through with love for her comrades, her stunning sisters, who would blame her? For a few like Jeannette, industrial America provided a paradoxical, companionable beauty.

It is my opinion that the photograph with which I began this story was taken at the height of such a spell. She had paused, abstracted from her work, hardly aware that she was out of her seat, staggered by an impossible longing. Had the camera been bold enough to hold its gaze, we would have seen her fall back against that column, her legs unsupporting.

But there was another important aspect of her personality, in fact the first to which I was introduced. When Franklin and I reached his tiny neat rooms on Chicago's south side, Jeannette had already arrived. There was a vague warm haze in the apartment. Cabbage, potatoes, and a dense reddish brick of meat boiled in the kitchen. As we stood in the open doorway, Jeannette's voice rushed to us. She was excited about something. "It's him," she called, "He's in the paper again. Our own Rosenwald." She came right up to us with her agitation before she noticed that Franklin was not alone. Then she dropped the newspaper to her side, looked directly at me and said, pleasantly, "Hello."

As you can see for yourself, Jeannette was a pretty woman. She was slender, vivid, pleasant, alive. Look at the photograph again. Do you see it? The charm, the vigor? And absolutely unafraid to be human. In an hour's time, what a range of conceptions could move across her face! Only a liar or a man who knew nothing of himself could fail to be impressed by her.

At any rate, Franklin quickly introduced us and as Jeannette took my coat she continued her eager story. It had to do with Mr. Rosenwald, whom I have already mentioned, Sears' president and genius, its animus. He was currently being questioned by the state senate's special committee of inquiry into the so-called "white slave trade." I knew a little about it and cared a little less, such scandals being in Dun about as real as the hunger of Chinese or the itch of foreign disease or some suffering thing else. I am one who, like many another American, is not easily moved by what does not confront him directly (and a sane attitude in an otherwise lunatic world that is).

"Look, darling, at what Rosenwald said today." She took unfirm Franklin affectionately by his arm. " 'I say the question of wages isn't a moral question.' Oh, I can hear him saying that, the reptile. 'It ought to be treated on an entirely different basis. I wouldn't combine the question of prostitution with wages. I say in my opinion there is no connection between the two.' " She read all this with her chest inflated in the way she imagined such a self-important swell as Mr. Rosenwald would do. Contradictorily, I noticed only how this gesture made taut the material of her blouse around her breasts.

"Do you know of the senate investigation?" she asked me as we began to eat our simple meal.

"I'm sorry. I know very little about it."

"Do you know why they are questioning Mr. Rosenwald?"

Another awkward no.

"Do you know what the women in Mr. Rosenwald's employ, women like myself, are paid? An average weekly wage of $9.12. Girls make only $8.00. And girls still living at home make only $5.00. Now, you don't make a lot of money, I know, but you've only just begun and already you make double even the highest of those figures. Do you think that's fair? And how do you imagine a girl would live on that salary? It's no wonder that the senators think that we have to turn to prostitution to survive." She smiled, gave a charming toss to her dark hair. "Of course, that's just their lurid imaginations. No one I know sells her body literally, although we sell ourselves to Rosenwald sure enough. But if the imagination of senators is what it takes to get Rosenwald to improve wages, I'm happy about it."

I didn't know it (it wouldn't come out for some time), but I was then meeting my first suffragist, an ally to famous Jane Addams of Hull House. Throughout Jeannette's vigorous talk Franklin only occasionally smiled and looked on her softly, fondly, loose leafy bits of cabbage hanging from his lips. They were together what God meant, or ought to have meant, in Adam and Eve: Adam a great, grey, soft fellow, incapable of malice; Eve small, quick, bright, full of the will to good.

Jeannette had more to say about her projects.

"I've even begun to organize some of the women at

Sears," she said, not bothering to control her enthusiasm for the idea. "I have thirteen now, and many of them older workers, who are willing to put their names to paper when the time is right." She was oblivious to the dinner. A bite of potato perched at the end of a slender fork in her extraordinarily delicate, articulate fingers. It was good food, but how much more delicious were those fingers! "And talking to my companions, it's all so sad. Those who say 'no' say 'no' only out of fear. They have children to feed. And those who say 'yes' are often so desperately desperate. There's one young girl who wants to move out on her own but can't because she's not paid enough. But she can't be paid more until she moves out. And while she's home her father takes rent from her wages, and uses her few hours off work as if she were the downstairs maid."

"Aren't you afraid you'll be found out and fired?" I asked.

"No," she responded. "But, in any event, with this senate investigation still cooking, Rosenwald is in no position to throw women out of work for protesting precisely what the senate investigates." She smiled cunningly. "In fact, dear Mr. Rosenwald seems to me just a bit vulnerable."

A few minutes later Franklin brought gracefully to the table a delicate, fluted decanter filled with a fascinating, bluish liqueur. He filled three tiny glasses and we drank. I talked about Dun and life in the country, and we drank. I was euphoric. Our cordials were more than cordial, more like humble miracles. Franklin asked about my parents; weren't they concerned about my life in the city?

"What do I know about my parents? What have they to do with me?" I answered.

Jeannette studied me. "You're either full of bluff or full of venom," she said.

I nodded nervously.

"Well, however your feelings about home, you are welcome in our house, such as it is," said Franklin. He covered my avid hand with his gentle generous paw. We drank.

Whatever I experienced that night, however euphoric, must have been doubled in a creature as keen as Jeannette. For late in the evening, at just the peak of our intoxication, she leaned toward Franklin, the warm blood filling her face, and whispered something. Then she got up, just a little awkwardly, and went to another room.

Now, I think it is easy enough to see that in matters that were political, social or economic, Jeannette was a sort of monster of philosophic rigor. She was awesome. The things she seemed to understand made me feel like the dunnish and downstate rube I most feared in myself. But in other matters (matters, I say to you, that were frankly sexual) she was contradictorily loaded with adolescent vulnerabilities. Surely you too have met women like this, women who can hold forth over lunch about the rights of women and the cruel stereotypes fostered by men, and then for the rest of the afternoon hound you about whether or not their waist is thick, their hair dull, or their complexion rough. Well, such a subtle dupe was Jeannette. All that she knew not to be was for her utterly real. Or at least this is how I explain what happened next.

There aren't many in these late days of the world who remember Fahreda Mahzar, Little Egypt, the queen of Chicago's streets of Cairo. But in 1913 she was still, or her memory was still, a presence. She was a dark-eyed Armenian minx who danced the hypnotizing hootchy-kootchy to the mournful sound of a flute. Well, silly as it sounds, when Jeannette returned Franklin began mumbling and murmuring vague, rhythmless woodwind sounds as Jeannette moved about in sequined jacket, pants, and veil. Frankly, she was about as plausible as one of those little prancing dogs that they put a skirt on and make to hop around on their brittle hind legs, except that no dog is serious. Jeannette was serious. That was part of her beauty and her vulnerability. Show me a human who doesn't want to be beautiful, to be desired, to have true sex, not the shallow, dusty imposter that you imagine in the beds of butchers, bankers, ward captains, and the other papery, transparent people you know. In short, Jeannette wished to be desired—even as Little Egypt was desired—and for the moment I thought she wished to be desired by me.

I was to see her dance many times, following many another meal in Franklin's apartment. There was always the entrancing, otherly look on her face, always the awkward, inventive angles of her arms and legs, always the happy, shimmering dimples in the small of her back like a thrilling mandala. A charm like no other dangling charm. And on most nights there was a reasonable conclusion. She'd drop from her trance, laugh at herself and us, sit down to coffee and more talk. She would hold our hands warmly, as if to thank us for indulging her, for being so understanding. It was as if she meant that this dancing, this business of sex, was necessary, perhaps crucial, but at the same time best not taken as serious, as more than merely personal.

But on that first giddy night, our blue liqueur rushing and radiating in her veins, she was one step beyond control, or perhaps one step or more into whatever human thing it is on the other side of control. Still rapt, still caught in that peculiar and changeable coma, she turned to us and began, I thought, to remove her blouse. I saw there a glimmer of bright, soft flesh. I knew right away that this wasn't what anyone expected (although I "expected" nothing) because Franklin was startled (and the startle reflex in a sea lion is no easy thing to trigger). But she caught herself before going, even by her own unconventional standards, too far. Then she looked at me. What did she see there? The confusion, thirst, and disloyalty of youth? I can't be certain. She stood gazing at me for some time until Franklin went to her (in embarrassment, in tenderness, in fatigue). He fastened her blouse as she said, "Isadora Duncan I'm not, darling." She then took his hand and they withdrew to an inner room, closing the door tightly behind.

In a few moments the great, breezy humpbacked

sighs of Franklin, our cetacean lover, drifted by. I put out the lights, curled up on the couch and was soon so gently put to sleep that I might have been at the sea's shore, cribbed in the sandy ocean's side.

* * *

The rest of my story can be told more quickly, being more like a fairy tale than anything real. At the end of my first quarter year with Sears, in the dead cold of December, I was unexpectedly called away from my desk one morning. I was taken down a series of gloomy corridors and led up stairs which, nonetheless, seemed to lead into the bowels of the great corporation. I was at last ordered into the private office of Julius Rosenwald. Three men sat in a circle of four chairs: my immediate supervisor, Mr. Heartfield, my Uncle Hiram and Julius Rosenwald himself. I was asked to take the fourth chair. As soon as I sat, Mr. Heartfield got up and began talking to me.

"We're sorry, young man, to take you away from your work this morning. And before I say a word about why we've asked you here I want you to know that it has nothing to do with the quality of your labor. We are all happy with you and in fact fully expect that you will rise quickly, perhaps in the next few weeks, from your present position.

"But on to other matters." Of course, he frowned, clasped his hands behind his back and paced as he said this. "As you no doubt have read in the papers, President Rosenwald has been working with the Illinois State

Senate about the problem of prostitution among young working women of our city. Mr. Rosenwald is certain that this is not a problem at Sears and he has said so. But he has pledged to the senators to act swiftly if he should learn of any lechery or vice in our company's midst. So let me ask you directly, young man, can you be of any help to Mr. Rosenwald? Do you know of any corrupt females in our employ?"

Being at that time as much an innocent eighteen-year-old as my true self, I could only blush and stammer, "No, of course not."

My Uncle Hiram set his face sternly and stared at me, tightening his hands around his knees.

Mr. Heartfield continued. "Your uncle has told us, young man, that you are familiar with"—he read from a sheet of paper—"Franklin X. and Jeannette G. Is that true?"

Well, then even I could see what this was all about. Of course I'd told Uncle Hiram of our soirees, told him again and again over a hundred idle cups of coffee, had stripped from Jeannette and Franklin ten times over everything except their flesh. But in front of this audience what I'd described for my uncle seemed like something I myself only knew from a dream.

It was then they brought in poor Franklin. With him they were brutal. They shook the sentences before him as if they were his guilt, as simple as ruin. "Do you share rooms with Miss G.?" "Is it true that you have brought this young man to your rooms for vicious purposes?" "No? Isn't it true that you brought Miss G. to Chicago, across state lines, from Buffalo?" "Do you know the penalty for interstate trafficking in prostitutes under the Mann Act?" And on and endlessly on.

Poor Franklin. When children are accused of some complicated misconduct, they strangle their fingers and disturb every muscle in their faces not out of any acknowledgement of guilt, but out of sheer panic, incomprehension, pure noodled confusion. Just so the great grey man. He was sent back to his desk. His yes or no wasn't needed anyway. They had what was enough for their purposes, a facsimile of blame.

Recall again our photographs. That one of Franklin, in which he stands more than stunned beside his desk (sonar gone, beached with a subtle disorder) was taken only moments after he was dismissed from Rosenwald's office. I believe that he has just noticed that the fragile vases of light hang delicately from the office ceiling like skulls at the end of fine, thin tethers. This makes sense to me considering the vast, sleek, seal-like figure which was found, the following week, pendent from the ceiling of his solitary apartment.

Deputies were sent for Jeannette, myself for some reason among them. But an alarm, we didn't know what, seemed to have preceded us down those halls. It was as if some shocking force went before us. And yet it had nothing to do with ourselves marching down that hall (natural though that would have been: we lacked only a goose step to be wholly Prussian). Apparently, something disturbing had happened in the great vault which held the quick young women who make a record of the customer's order. I wanted to run, catch her before she harmed her cause, catch her before she harmed ours, I wasn't sure which. And I was right about it being her—it was Jeannette, she had found out about our meeting, somehow, from someone, perhaps from one of her thirteen signed up for Reform.

We at last turned the corner into the hall where she worked. And there was the reason for the commotion: Jeannette sat at her desk working carefully. Typing. But she had removed her blouse and the light corseting slip which she wore to her job, and she was allowing to pause, brightly above the keys of her typewriter, her breasts. Yes, of course, my heart went out to her. I knew she was no immodest slattern, no drunken, blowsy madwoman. I alone understood that now at last she had become the heroic Isadora! It was an inspired, yet desperate effort to save herself, to organize and make militant her co-workers. And in fact I do sincerely believe that her ploy came near to frustrating the enormous power that we (the guards and myself) represented. As we stood at the top of the aisle in which she sat, she looked up from her work and caught the eye of every woman near her. She was furious. Then she stood and said, "This is it, my friends. They'll make an example of me. Well, if I'm to be called a prostitute, at least I look the part." Now, if every one of those women had turned then to every other woman in proximity, why—Lord!—rebellion would have multiplied like a strange new kind of wealth. They might all have followed her lead. Imagine a thousand breasts instantly smiling above the brilliant typewriters!

Well, I saw dozens of agitated fingers trembling around necklines. Of course, as soon as this became conscious it was translated up the neck into a frantic pulling and scraping. Someone complained of the heat, another actually fainted. And of course, Jeannette was left alone. The moment had passed. My two security friends rushed at her and tried to force her clothing back around her chest. I couldn't help but see that in the process their sordid, toad-like fingers bruised her.

Ultimately, we led her out of the Sears building into the streets, to be taken to the police, to be charged with indecent exposure, riotous conduct, prostitution, other crimes against the people of Illinois. But at the very first corner we met one of the city's beggars, an old woman with a box of apples, who only hoped that by the end of the day she could afford to wrap herself with newspaper and thus keep from freezing to death for another night. But she wore a large, comical, flapping black hat that made her look like a sorceress or a witch from a children's tale. As we passed her, she rushed out and took Jeannette by the arm. "Here, lady, buy an apple of me," she said, pulling Jeannette back toward her crate.

"No, old woman," Jeannette said sadly. "I have no money for you."

"Well then God bless you, lady, take one free." And she handed her an apple.

In her hand the apple fell neatly into two perfectly separated halves. "Oh, I know it's tedious and tiresome. We ladies are always being handed fruit or flowers. But look you, an apple is a beautiful thing." They studied the fascinating chambers of the core. "This seed looks to me as hard and glossy as the shell of a lac bug."

"And here, you men," the old girl had us all now, "something for you." She was a lunatic. She handed to the security men green balls, bedunged, fungal, which when placed in their hands unfurled with a fetid slap. "There you are," she crooned. "Whosoever of you returns in one year and has most caused to multiply what you have been given, you can keep it all for yourselves, if you want." She laughed in a way that frightened me. "Or you can take my place here on the corner." More laughter. "I tell you what, you can go to a baseball game. There you are. Now get ye, get ye."

The guards went off with their captive, wiping their hands against their pants legs, cursing, perhaps planning to return for the crone. Rid the streets of another excrescence. But she still had me by the arm with those old, clutching fingers strong as roots. "Young man, I can see that you are the one who cares for her. Well, then, mark my words, don't let them take her into that building yonder. They beat women in that building. I saw them take a nice young woman in there last week, but when she came out she had a beak, and she was all fiberlike and episcopal. And here, young man—something for you." She put a garish copper penny of a terrifying and alien coinage in my palm.

* * *

Let me ask you a question, a moral question, on which I would like to put as fine a point as I possibly can.

Ought one to judge people on the basis of one's own experience or on others' experience? Who is of so slavish a nature— so at heart un-American—that he would say, "Let others judge in my place. I abstain"? Well, how then could I fail to see Sears, Julius Rosenwald, my uncle, and even the great City of Doubt in anything but a positive light? A place was made for me. I was clapped to a bosom. Made welcome. Allowed to rise, to multiply, to prosper. What *experience* had I with which to prop any resentment? I'm no ingrate; rather, I'm fiendishly loyal. And so I venerate the austere figure of Rosenwald as a father, teacher, provider.

If Franklin is now dead, it is by his own hand, his own doing. If Jeannette lives in despair, regret, poverty, shame, that is a matter so perplexed, a problem so knotted in uncertainty that a man would be a fool to pause before that Medusa's regard. Better to get on with the business of life.

You've Changed

Our killer stands at the corner of State and Semper Dolens. A bloody carnation, of florid petal, blossoms from his vicious kisser.

My name is Rita. I sing scat with Tony D's Big Band at the Stop Time hot spot, tops here in Fargo. Or sang. When there was a Tony D. Time is tough.

For a while, the pictures the club took of us up on the bandstand gave our man a turn. Tony didn't look dead in those. See, he's in his little crouch, limpid to the beat, his baton as apparent as Duke's used to be. Looking back over his shoulder at me, he smiles, keen about the music, avid about the way I look. And I do look fine, I can see it in his eyes. I've got on black pumps so I can take a step when I need to, silks like brass, a dress that billows when it's supposed to, bare shoulders that kill 'em, hair that comes down so pretty like June Christy's did. And every boy out there, every boy back from the wars, loved me. And I know Tony loved me. Loved me like no other. But now it's gone; gone the romance that filled my heart. It was just like a flame. Yes it was. Love burned brightly then became an empty shadow.

After we played, Tony and I would go back to my

place, a one-room in Shatter's Hotel, with the neon SHATTERS lighting the whole place. We'd get some ice and a bottle of booze and become marvelous things until the sun came up. Tony was a good Italian boy from Chicago. He knew how to make love so it hurt if he wanted, but he never wanted. He was point of fact worried about my fun.

But those in the know complain about the game he played with the strawberries and the bullets. Like, if he was just some wise guy, I'd have been our killer to him myself, years before nature's boy did the trick. Anyhow, regarding my funny man, he put three of each inside me, see. Then he'd nose around to find them. The strawberries he'd chew and let the juices creep down his chin. Then he'd bewilder my thighs with some kisses. The bullets he'd gobble and spit out racketing on the floor. Then for the rest of my life every time I walk through the room I have to listen to cartridges carom over the hardwood. Even now I'll sometimes find one propped in a corner like a monument.

And so it could have gone on for us for a while. It did go on for a while. I get confused. What do we lovers expect? This love of mine goes on and on, I can tell you. In the little hours of the morning, I lie awake and think about that boy. I'd be his again, if only he would call.

That other fella must have been standing out on the fire escape the whole time. I'll bet that's what it was. And I bet he heard every word we said. Like:

"I think that if a girl really loves someone, she loves all his smells."

"You said it. Smell this hand."

"Right!"

"I'll clean it Tuesday. After that I don't believe it's polite."

The fact that killer-diller overheard our courtesies, sitting in himself out there, makes my blood boil.

To tell the truth, I'd heard of others meeting a man as bad as our man. It happened to a friend of a friend and others read about it in the paper for sure. This story happened in Topeka. Elsie and Alta were two girls on their own for the first time. They fled farm families and the misery of a clapboard house. I know, for a different misery you say, smart guy. Well, they got themselves a nice house to share on 7th Avenue, got part-time jobs at the Bijou and Myrtle's Donut Divan, did the clubs at night, met boys, did what they wanted. So, one evening close to dawn they're walking back from Mort's Shangri La doing girl talk when this big, dark man starts following them. They walk a little faster. Can't you hear their high heels smacking and their brittle ankles snapping? So finally they're half a block from home and he's running after them, and they're running stride for stride, knocking elbows, panting, hair in the face. At last they get to their door and get inside and shut it tight. Just in time, by God. Still, the bad man presses his face against the window—a filthy thing, mixed up, not a believable face at all—and he only says two words, "Bloody murder!!"

Well, Elsie and Alta try not to think about it, although they've been plenty bad scared. In the next week a lot of nights were especially dark and windy with rain threatening. Egg yolks were green and turned black in the pan. Then they hear on the radio how a lunatic killer has escaped from a local criminal asylum and may be hiding out in town.

So the girls stop going out after dark and just stay home playing Scrabble and listening to the Scarlet Pimpernel on the radio and eating plates of black fudge. Then one night they get a phone call and Elsie answers it. But all she hears is a man's sick laugh. Later they get another call from Mr. Funny-bones and this time the girls are scared. Elsie decides to call the operator for help, but Alta says, "Honey, you handle this. I'm going upstairs to bed and pull the covers over my head." So okay this is really moving now, the operator instructs Elsie to keep the caller on the line so she can trace the call. Shortly, the telephone rings again and Elsie answers and keeps the Good-Humor Man on the line for a time. Within a few minutes, the operator calls back telling Elsie to leave the house immediately because she has traced the call to an upstairs phone.

Elsie hangs up and runs to the stairway to call Alta. But she hears a thumping sound coming from the stairway and when she approaches the stairs she sees her friend dragging herself down by her chin, all of her limbs cut off from her body. Boy.

Now, regarding my case, I know not all of you are sympathetic. You think jazz musicians get what's coming to them. I tell you Tony D. was an angel and you say, yeah, you got angels and rhythmic beasts confused. You say, fact: the man kept company with mobsters. A big night for him was when a murderer would tip a hundred bucks to hear "It's Tight Like That." Sweetheart, you make the devil's deal, you pay the devil's price. Remember the night the orchestra played "Gut Bucket" and the saxophone section convulsed in the middle of a break, their faces black and their tongues poking out? The crowd loved it.

What's there to say? We had to play our music and we had to eat. The Church of Latter Day Saints didn't offer to pick up the check, so we had to choose our friends from the friendly. I keep hearing how bad the gangsters were. All I can say is that I wish I was still working for them. They had guts, they didn't want no beer hall *lieder*, no ballads of Katy O'Day. They wanted to dance rough and dirty with no coats on and their suspenders down. They wanted the real thing, something with ESSence.

Still, there's that night like no other, when I lost my lover man. I went down to the corner to get him some knuckles and a bottle of beer. But when I came back he was stretched out on the bed in his socks and garters (like he was dressing and getting ready to leave? break my heart?) In the middle of his forehead was a leaky rose bud. And on his chest, tacked to his sternum, was a note which read, "You don't waltz on the Big Guy, Jack." I felt pretty bad. I sat down next to him and said, "Darling, you've changed. That sparkle in your eyes is gone. Your smile is just a careless yawn. You're breaking my heart. Yes, you've changed. Your kisses now are so blase. You're bored with me in every way. I can't understand why you've changed."

* * *

". . . And that's the kind of magic music we made with our lips. When we kissed." Those were among my first words to Inspector Vincent Barocco. He didn't take them down in his little notebook, though. Well, he said he wanted the facts about my relationship to Tony. So I was giving him the facts. Guess he thought it was kind of strange.

But nothing I did or could have done, thought or might have thought, could ever have been as strange as the inspector himself. He didn't come see me until Tony was taken away, the little puddles of blood mopped up and the world made to seem as if he'd never been at all. (But like those folks who lose an arm yet feel their fingers twitching in space, I could feel his sweet hands at my hips, his tongue tender between my lips.) The first words Mr. Barocco said to me—no bad chance, tough luck sentiment from this guy—were, "May I use your telephone?"

I imagined it must have been some urgent police business so I said okay. But he stayed on the phone for forty-five minutes, long distance to Detroit City, Michigan, where his sister lived. I'd have said something about the rates, but I felt sorry for him. As he talked, he turned grey and his head sank unsupportable to his knees. He paused now and then to put the receiver down and cry into a bright plaid handkerchief of flannel.

Soon enough, there I was, of course, holding that tough guy in my arms as he talked, rocking him now and then to let him know someone still cared.

Well, it seemed that his sister had suddenly taken ill and died. You know how bad the water is getting in our cities. Apparently, the girl swallowed some fearsome spawn. An octopus grew inside her reaching to every part of her body, finally splitting right through her skin. Mr. Barocco got the facts from his auntie.

The story made me think. What spores have I swallowed? Is something hatching inside of me? A girl shouldn't touch water, teeming like a city, if she's not prepared to give birth to and then provide the tit for a monster.

Well, enough is enough even for a cop who is used to long hours and bad news. My problems could wait till morning. So I took him over to my bed and put him under the covers. I opened my blouse just a little so he could sleep with his head on my breast. The nice guys are just like babies and appreciate such kindnesses from women. Do that for any of the rest of them and you'll wake up with a hole chewed through you, as if you'd snuggled with a starving rat.

As with most of the rest of us, it's hard for me to tell my life's blessings from its curses. It has surely been my good luck that the loss of every beautiful, desirable man has been followed by the arrival of another just as loveable. Desire is an express train without a terminal. You roar through the countryside, rattle over the rails, but you don't ever quite arrive. St. Lou? Nope. Kansas City? Not that, either. Not that, not that. Might as well find a seat in the club car and settle back.

Which in its contrary way makes it all not quite so contrary. I don't have now any of the men I've ever wanted. I'm not happy. But the point I'm making is, we lovers don't really want what we want so badly we'd die for it. We desire not having what we desire. No news in this. I guess I'm just saying that this logic makes me about the most gratified person in the world. Lucky me.

Vinnie Barocco was one good-looking man. He dressed nice too, not like a cop. Pleated pants and expensive jackets. Imported shoes. And his dark hair lay back so soft and smooth, like a Neapolitan torch singer. I mean, I only had to take one look at him to hear the heart's throb of the conga drums. Fandango, cha-cha, tango: The man touched me where I lived.

The next morning Vincent and I sat in the kitchen. When he got up for some coffee, I watched his body move so smooth beneath his clothes. Once my hand went, in inspiration, between my breasts to a little pearl of his saliva, what he'd drooled childishly in his sleep. I wanted to kiss him so bad that morning. Let him taste the force of my spit. But I didn't want to scare him.

And he was scareable. For all his beauty and strength, you could see in his eyes that this was a man who was always sad. And it wasn't just his sister's galling death. It was an infirmity in his blood. So, though I knew I wanted him, wanted to love him like no other, I knew it wouldn't be easy.

"Rita," he said to me, "It's certain that your friend Tony's death was a mob job. We're fairly sure that the killer stood out on the fire escape waiting for his opportunity. When you left, he came in through the window and shot Mr. D. once in the forehead with a Smith and Wesson .38 caliber handgun. Standard execution modus for one of the local gangs."

I licked a bit of berry jam off a tiny silver spoon. The news, the little spoon, the sweetness of the jam, it all made me feel so sad. I got all choked up. "Will you be able to get the guy who did it?" I asked.

Vinnie, he reached a hand across the table and took mine, returning the care I had shown him earlier. He had so much to be busted up about, too. You should have seen the tenderness in those cool, dark eyes. "Honey, we know who did it. He's death's big boy in these parts. I don't know how many men he's killed, but he's killed enough. The locals just call him Brute. Or Buster. The problem is proving he did it."

"Can't you just find some evidence?"

Vincent sat back, nodded and then said, "Think about it, Rita. There are no witnesses, the motive died with Tony, the killer will have an alibi, and there are no fingerprints, no marks, not a single physical clue. What kind of case could we make?"

A little later, Inspector Barocco left me alone in my rooms.

As they say, life is full of surprises. I was preparing myself for what I thought would be one of the loneliest nights of my life. Every time I looked at something Tony had touched or a book he had read, I'd start to shake, bad scared. It wasn't that I feared the return of our killer. To tell you the truth, I was so low that if the Hatchet-man had come I think I would have found him sweet and embraceable. And it certainly wasn't that I feared Tony's haunting, blue return. It was more that I knew my life was going to go on for a long while yet, but I had no idea what was going to happen to me. On some unknowable Wednesday, would I be afflicted with a humiliating dysfunction? "Miss Rita, I'm sorry. Your liver is now pure malignance. It has metamorphosed weirdly. X-rays show it now to be a large but rather cramped amphibian. If you put your hand here you can feel where its snout pushes against your abdomen. See? What we don't know at this point is whether he will sit there and merely refuse obstinately to consider a liver's important duties, or if he will turn more malicious and begin to chew at other neighbor organs. Is there anyone we can contact for you? You have at least another half-hour to live."

Well, I was just getting ready to ask a bottle of Gordon's gin to put me out, when there was a knock at the door. I opened it quickly, wanton to fate. And there, delight to my eyes, was Inspector Vincent Barocco, tuxedoed, slicked, cologned and with a bright spring bouquet in his hand.

"I was hoping you might like to go out to dinner," he said. "Then maybe the Tiara Ballroom after for dancing."

People, when I hear it said, regarding Fargo, that there is better livin' elsewhere, I say, "Go your way to that better livin'." Because that night Fargo was heaven. We started with dinner, rich filets wrapped in sweet bacon. Couple bottles of wine. Then to the ballroom for dancing. Red Nichols was in town. Man, we cut a rug. That band could flat swing. Then late in the evening they played some slow tunes to get people in the precise mood for a cozy drive home. The Inspector's leg slipped between my legs, and the rubbing against my silk stockings nearly made me sane. Then I felt him hard against my belly. He kissed me right there on the floor, tongue and all. And I said, this is it, *this* is what I want from life.

* * *

Next thing, it was morning. I opened my eyes and there across the room was the beautiful back, the perfect long legs of my new thrill. God knows, we'd probably gotten only a couple hours of sleep, but right away I wanted him again. He did something to me. Sent chills right through me. So I made a little whistle and threw back the covers. Get an eyeful of this, fella.

Vincent gave one of his pretty smiles and came over. He got in bed and we were just rollin' over, getting ready to slice some bacon, when a horrible thing happened. It was as if a dead rat, horrid black thing, had fallen between us. Vincent jumped back, shocked. He was limp as misery, poor guy. Bully-boy gone.

In fact, when I rolled over a matchbook had appeared

applied to my thigh, grafted there, leeching to the moist skin. It was scarlet with black lettering. I took it delicately in my fingers and ripped it away.

> THE SEA WOLF
> A NIGHT SPOT
> FARGO'S FINEST OYSTER BAR

Well, I was damned curious to look at the thing, so I did. And what do you know, on the inside was scratched the name of that murderous roustabout, our mutual killer: BUSTER.

I looked at Vincent and smiled. "Your evidence, Inspector."

I couldn't get Vincent to smile, though. He turned so pale it was like he'd become one with the light in the room. Become a high-frequency buzz and vanished. I pulled the handkerchief from his suit pocket and carefully wrapped the matchbook. Might be some fingerprints on it, then what we'd have would be even more than circumstantial. We'd nail the lousy bastard, that fuck. He'd rue the day.

"We're going to get that creep, aren't we, Vincent? We can do it. Then we'll go away, just the two of us. Nevada maybe. I know some guys out there who can fix me up in a club. It'll be good times. What do you think?" But the Inspector didn't seem to be doing much thinking. The last few moments had seen the arrival of an addling complexity for him. He looked vague. He tried to wedge a shoe on the wrong foot. I had to go over, straighten out his socks, warm his feet in my lap and only then dare to slip his shoes on. He'd changed. He was not the angel I once knew. He was nervous. He was dying to leave.

I said, "What's the matter, sweetheart?"

He couldn't even look me in the eye. Love 'em and leave 'em, was that it, Wisenheimer? "Yes," he said, "this is the break we've been waiting for. I've had a swell time." He walked around the room getting his coat and stuff. "You can be sure I'll be in touch. This new information is important, bet your life. I think Mr. Brute has gone a step too far this time. I don't think he knows with whom he's fooling. Nevada sounds great. Understand it's pretty this time of year. And you're wonderful, the best, kid, really, bee's knees. I think his pals will be in for a big surprise to see his hide nailed to the barn door. And maybe we can get hitched some day. How's that sound? Then get away from here, like you say. Beat the birds down to Acapulco. Course we got to be darned careful 'bout this new information. Judge is gonna want to see that all's in order. I mean, what if this is a plant? What if the poor slob is being set up? It happens, you know. Not that anyone would think you did it. No sir, you're tops, kid. Top of the tops. I can testify to that. But this is all happening so fast. I tell ya, my head is spinning. Baby, it must be love. I'm getting dizzy in my knees. Let me put it this way, sugar, I just need some time to myself to think this thing through. You understand, don't you, kiddo? I mean, this is important stuff. The boys in the lab are going to want to look at it long and hard. The crime has got to fit our man like a Trojan. Ha ha. Then it'll be just you and me. All the way! Zoom! No kidding, gonna be terrific, just give me a couple of weeks to make the pieces fit. Nothing wrong with that, is there? I mean, I'm human, baby, nothing has changed, I just need some breathing room. Okay?"

I had to think hard to remember the sweet man with whom I'd spent the night. I wanted to be able to trust him. If I couldn't I'd take a razor to his lips. Open them like you do the flesh of a peach. He'd never kiss again. I'd save another poor girl from being used. But then, maybe he would come through for me. I really do believe he was a good guy at heart. He was just scared, as who wouldn't be. He was going to have to go nose-to-nose with the mob. A relaxing prospect for no one. What can I say? I was in love with the guy. He'd come straight. So I brought him to the door and kissed him goodbye. "Do what's best for us, sweetheart," I said.

After about a week, I decided to call.

"Fargo police. Officer Foulpole speaking."

"I'm trying to get in touch with Inspector Vincent Barocco, homicide. Can you connect me?"

A long perplexing pause.

"Hello? Officer Foulpole?"

"Just a moment. I'm remembering something."

"What?"

"What you said reminded me of something. What is your name by the way?"

"Rita."

"Rita. Nice name. Hey, you're the singer, right? Friend to Tony D. who went and got himself knocked off by the mob, right? Say, I love your act. Me and my girlfriend caught you couple weeks ago at the Stop Time."

"Thanks, honey."

"Anyway, when you mentioned Barocco, I remembered that I had a dream about him just last night. It was kind of weird, but I guess that's what dreams are for, so you can think about all of the weird things that might come to you. What happened was that Barocco and I were in this big opera hall, see. A real old one, with lots of carved stone and corridors going nowhere and monstrous geeks with horrible mouths dripping from the walls. So Barocco says to me, 'We're going to play a game, Foulpole. You and me. It's called "I kill you, you kill me." With guns. Now you go hide. I'll give you thirty seconds.' Well, I'm scared to death, right? I mean, I just answer the phone around here and Barocco's this big deal in homicide. Probably killed a hundred men.

"Next thing, I'm ducking down behind some chairs in the balcony of the opera hall. Right down by the rail. In comes Barocco in evening wear with this beautiful dish. And it's like he's completely forgotten the game. He's just talking and taking off his scarf and gonna sit down and listen to the music. So, what the hell, I pop up with this fantastic gun, an automatic pistol, that squeezes off bullets so fast, just like turning on electric lights. But Barocco sees me just in time and he reaches in his coat for his gun. But when he pulls it out, it's this fiesty weasel and, man, it locks those sharp little teeth into his hand, into that web of skin between the thumb and first finger.

"Anyhow, I pull off three shots—wham, wham, wham—and down he goes. I run over and find he's got one bullet in his shoulder. The other two missed. I'm apologetic as hell. I didn't really want to play the game, I say, it was his idea. And he says it's all right. I did a good job. Can I get him to a doctor? So me and his girl pick him up and carry him out of the place and get a taxi. End dream."

I thought about this for a second, then said, "Do you always tell people about your dreams, Mr. Foulpole?"

"When they're relevant. What am I supposed to do? Pretend they never happened?"

* * *

It all happened on Friday, March the 15th, 1955. I hadn't seen or heard from Vinnie in a month. The "case" was nowhere. According to what information I could get from local humor like Foulpole, the investigation was still open and being directed by Barocco, but the Inspector was on leave doing research. When I asked where on leave, I was told just "left on leave." When I asked what the point of the research was, I was told, "Expect anything."

In spite of all this, my work, my singing, was getting stranger and more beautiful. An ill wind moved against me—like some sick, warm southerly—but I took it in, inspired it, and when I breathed it back out it was sad maybe but you could find love in it.

But as I say, on the 15th of March something happened. It was about eleven o'clock, I hadn't been up long,

I was drinking some coffee. Then, there was a knock at the door. And what do you think, it was our killer. He stood there, his face pink and raw like pig meat, his grin peeking through like the white bone in a rack of ribs. "Well," I said, "If it ain't Mr. Buster Moribundi. What's shakin', Jake?"

Like it is with these thugs, he said nothing. Strong and silent! What a riot. "So what are you gonna do? Kill me? Here it is—my heart. No bigger than a pippin. Pick it up, fat boy. May it serve you well."

I had him pegged and he knew it, but he was committed to his methods. He stepped in and held out a letter, addressed to me, postmarked Taos, New Mexico.

"Mail call."

I was frightened, of course, and eager to see what was what. So I took the letter, ripped a finger through a fold and read.

> My dear Rita:
>
> Picture this: I'm spread out on one of those porcelain tables at the city morgue. That lame-brain Larry Biparous is lookin' me over and making a mess of the whole process like usual. I probably got a steak knife sticking in my heart with the words "Eat chiles relenos in Rawlins, Wyoming" on the handle. But Lawrence don't care, he's got to crack the big nut so he can thin-slice the pink stuff like prosciutto. I can't let me die! Decorum counts for nothin' with the guys we hire to handle the dead. They're into cross sections only. They think the designs are pretty. Biparous has

got some on the wall of his den.

But really, sweetheart, I miss you so. And I am going to take care of you, too. I'm giving fair warning, that goon Brute keeps nosin' round, I'm gonna bust his noggin. It's just that these subtle matters are better considered in the dark. I know I could have hung around Fargo for months applying the magnifying glass of routine to these issues, but it would have got us nowhere. Here, in Taos, I fly by night, scrutinize the implications of "The Sea Wolf" under Mrs. Eve Brat's HOP INN neon. "Fargo's Finest Oysters"—a conundrumic rune, what?

But to tell you the truth, I could give a fuck about Tony. What I really want to know is why do I have to feel so bad, in myself? And why do terrible things keep happening to me? And why don't you abandon the rest of your life in order to make me feel just a little better? But don't try finding me here in Taos. Tomorrow, I'm gone. Somewhere great, Flagstaff mebbe.

>I'll always love you,
>Inspector Vincent Barocco

When I looked up from my lover's letter (and he *was* my lover—no one had ever loved me like he had—I knew it in one night), I saw that Brute's grin had become a sort of hedgehog's chuckle. I even thought he was going to speak. He did.

"So, honey bunch," he said, kinda pushin' the brim of his fedora back, making room on his face for something to happen. "Howsabouta little kiss." He leaned over me and from his yap issued the mean smell of a thousand years of undigested fish life. The inside of his mouth and throat were lined with glistening scales which slid all the way down a gruesome cleft to his heart. Well, this girl don't cater to fresh guys, let alone to this kind of rotten fresh guy. So—pow—I let him have it right in the kisser. Funny thing, though, the force of it made his puckered lips spread like a meaty blossom. It was like I'd punched something very soft: It would never be a mouth again. I mean, it was so much what I hadn't expected that I laughed. So, old Bluster, he turned and ran "wee,wee,wee" all the way home.

Well, until that moment I never knew what love could do. I roused myself—the chestnuts were in blossom, crocuses reaching with their hungry scalloped mouths—and put on a wide spring dress. I packed a little bag and walked off in perfect weather to catch a bus south. I was going to find Vince for good. 'Cause he's my guy. I know he'll always be. And I will try to keep him lovin' me. He's careless about me, I don't think he tries. But once in a while he'll hug me and smile. And I can see me in his eyes.

Howdy Doody Is Dead

An apocryphalyptic fairy tale

In the Peanut Gallery, the children boiled. Loaves of Wonder Bread, Hostess Cupcakes, Tootsie Rolls like tidy feces spilled out from beneath the bleachers. A side stage door strained and trembled. That was the last day. I, Doctory Ditto, a simple toymaker and one of Howdy's innumerable fathers, was left the sorry task of relating just how it had all come to pass. This, you must take my word, is a true story, although none remain to bear me witness.

It was once upon a time and it was December 27, 1941. It was in a faraway land that was once known as California. Another Howard was born to parents. I am able to show you many photographs of the boy, taken with the family Brownie. The edges are serrated, someone's idea of decoration. For in the '40s whatever was not grossly functional, baldly machine fit, was ipso facto decorative. Let me tell you, even children's toys acquired a charmless generality. No more could you take a leg of wood and stout knife and whittle until a great pal, a hero, or the shifting self of the devil surfaced. This fact we should have known to be a sign. Searching the

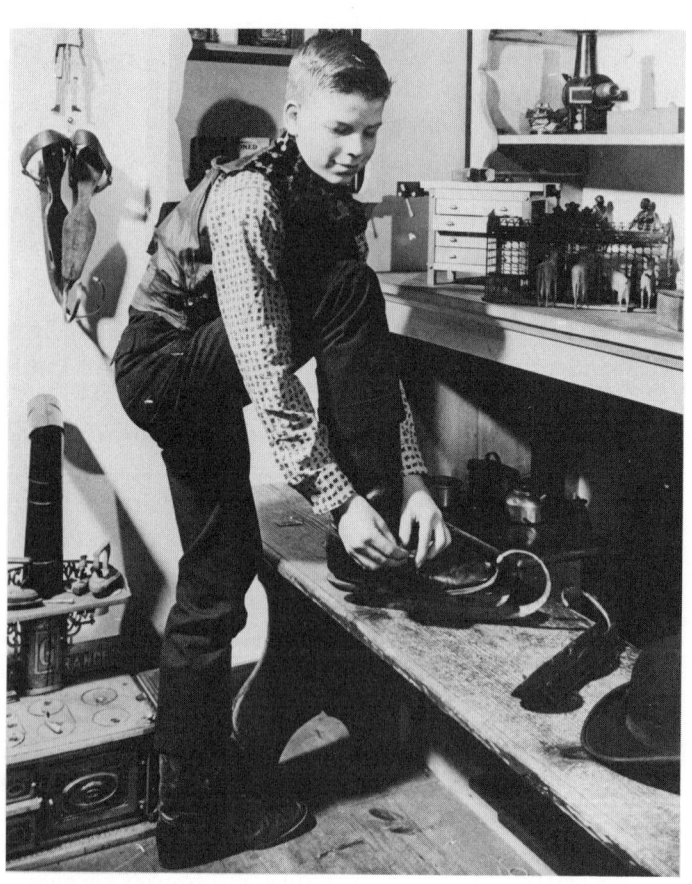

depraved void in the Barbie's eyes, seeing there that cruel and sterile lust, we should have understood, we should have been able to see more clearly the shape of things.

Nevertheless, there is something for us in these early photos of Howard. They are crisp, glossy, black-and-white, precisely what I need in my effort to make what is simply true seem at the very least plausible. Here, for example, is one of our boy on his tricycle. The cowboy hat hung behind the head is a nice touch, don't you think? There's the Cisco Kid in that. And look here, he's smoking a pipe with his dad. Or making the stranger dance with his six- shooter. But what in the world do I expect you to make of all this? Why, it's the chemistry! Add together a driveway, a concrete sidewalk, a newly planted lawn, a nice quiet suburb, a boy who thinks he's the son of Hopalong Cassidy, who hasn't a clue that he's not a real boy at all, and above everything a queer half-light, as if the sun were the light bulb in a refrigerator. What the poor boy doesn't understand is enough to make you weep.

But, you say, am I not a bit ahead of myself? What about Howard's mom and dad? Who were they? How did they bring Howard about? How does this information help to explain his tragic character? Well, I'm sorry to say that I'm not sure what needs to be known about his parents, since they were out of his life by the time he was six. Sure! He had his own show by then, 1947.

LET'S GIVE A ROUSING CHEER, 'CAUSE HOWDY DOODY'S HERE.

I will say, though, that if his father had known that he carried the germ of such a one as son-Howard, he might have given another thought to what he was about as he clambered over Mom's nice big backside, sturdy as baking soda biscuits.

When Dad met Mom, it was April of 1941, the last spring before the war, and it was San Diego, California, the naval facility there. Dad was a strapping lad of a man, born in wheat's home, Kansas. He played varsity sports in the public schools, learned to smoke Lucky Strikes while walking the long country roads to class, and when a lightning storm was near, and ozone in the air met with the Dixie Peach in his hair, he seemed to radiate. He was a "plumb enchanted guy," so the girls all said.

But Kansas couldn't hold him. A month after graduation, he was off to join the navy and see exotic ports of call: Pearl Harbor, San Diego, Alameda. That's how he came to meet Wanda, Howard's mom, some three years later, near the end of his hitch, in palpable, palmy, remorseless San Diego. Now, Wanda too was a child of the farm, but she was also part of a new American type. She had rejected the ground worn bare by the scratching of chickens, and rejected the sparse shade of an oak. She came to San Diego to take a job in a parts factory in war-related industry. But she would stay because of the life that flowed from the folds and flounces beneath San Diego's tropical skirt. San Diego acted on her as if it were the most acceptable hand come to hunch permanently at her groin. It was a change, as different from her former life as a moan from a yawn, and it was something she would never willingly forsake.

Wanda was a May Queen with a lunch box. She was an eyeful that knew it. And she was a meat eater. Learning the various purposes of a wrench had changed her; it had changed the way she approached a pork chop. To see the way she held the teed bone and plucked the grey meat from it, a man had to be completely cocksure to ask if maybe there wasn't just one bite on it somewhere for himself.

But a country boy like Howard's dad didn't know enough to be daunted by Wanda. So one warm spring night, at Uncle Chuck's Bar and Grill, where Wanda ate her chops and drank plenty of vodka in grapefruit juice, Dad pulled up a chair. But, jeez, he was something special himself. He took off his sailor's hat and puffed on his Lucky, made it blaze in that dim space like a tiny red eye. Then he reached across and gripped Wanda's hand, which gripped the greasy pork chop. Then he brought the whole thing, hand, chop and all, over to his own lips and sunk his teeth into the meat firmly, painfully, splendidly. A correlative chunk of Wanda's thigh trembled, felt the sweet nip of it.

It was not very much later that they were in the backseat of a 1936 Buick convertible, stars overhead, Dad over Mom, larding each other with kisses, comforting each other with juices that this poor toysmith can do no justice to. And you know what? Something special happened, too. Little Howdy was conceived that night.

Soon the war was over (or over for Dad, who had the

good fortune to be gettin' out when the gettin' was good, just when a million others were having to join during the very scorch of it) and Mom and Dad got married. Dad found a job adjusting claims that a world of people made against his employer. Eager to better himself, provide for his family, buy ball bats for his boy, Dad went to night school where he learned about engineering, geography, the basics of accounting and field tactics. On the weekends he took apart radios, planted lawns, cleaned the Buick's carburator, and threw baseballs that always came caroming off of Howdy's dense hands. But never, never did he look in Wanda's eyes, for fear of what obscure thing he might find fermenting in that bright liquid.

* * *

If it's possible for five years to be a moment, Wanda spent 1941-46 in one long, slow startle, in which painfully, gradually she demanded, "Hey, Buster Brown, what's happening here?" What had happened was that she was now a wife and mother and no longer responsible for her own keeping. It seemed to her that getting married had been a trade. In exchange for a son, she had given up her tough, hungry life of busses, sandwiches made with Bob Ostrow luncheon meats, the smell of machines, the exciting smell of men at work, men jitterbugging, men hot and hepped with Burgermeister beer and Old Crow whiskey. But now, after all, she could watch TV.

One day after watching a program on which a woman

won seven Amana gas ranges and a weekend for two in Oakland, she took the front door off its hinges, dragged it out into the yard, buttered it high and low with Sterno and set it on fire. Little Howdy went teetering after her on his uncertain legs, trusting that there was something to be learned in all this. The door was still smoldering when her husband came home. The fire captain was not happy and talked to Howard's dad man to man.

The next day Wanda took all of the canned goods and produce and frozen meats and cartons of milk, put them in the Sears' Best Kenmore oven and turned it on Broil. Later she said she would have done something, would have tried to save the day, but her fingers had gotten tangled in her hair. This time the fire captain took Dad aside and laid it on the line.

The ultimate day, the fateful day was hung with a suspicious ordinariness. When Dad came home from work, Wanda greeted him at the new green-enameled front door. Her hair was combed, she was neat, she wore a house dress open nearly to her waist, she had a Chef Boyardee genuine gourmet Italian dinner prepared. Dad didn't like the looks of it. It was like in the cowboy movies when things are quiet, too quiet.

"Where's Howard?" he asked.

"He's all right. He's in his bedroom."

"Why doesn't he come out to give me a kiss?"

"I've hung him up in his closet."

Dad ran down the hall. He'd save his boy if he could. But when he reached the bedroom, sure enough, there was Howdy, strung up by a noose of stiff box-cord suspended from a hook for hanging garments high up the closet door.

Coming up behind, Mother said, with some annoyance, "Now look what you've made me do."

It was this awful experience that demonstrated beyond doubt that Howdy was not like other boys. He survived his own hanging because he was a woodenhead, a puppet, a marionette; and as everyone knows, a puppet cannot be hung, except in the sense that puppets are routinely bestrung.

As for murderous Mom and mortified Dad, Howdy's last memories of them are of a distant, indistinct wrangling. Howdy was systematically orphaned. That is, as his parents willed themselves to eternal mutual recrimination before an indefinite series of drowsy magistrates, Howdy was—for his own well-being and protection—taken off and put in the mothering care of programs, organizations, funds, resources, out-reaches, etc. And, the truth be told, things didn't go badly for the youngster. Buffalo Bob Smith was appointed as his guardian, and within just a few months a Saturday morning television show, of which he was the star and host, was on the air. Best of all, in 1958 a love relationship, which had long been growing, declared itself. Howdy and the Story Princess announced their engagement and a sensible marriage date for the spring of 1962. The Princess was a longtime member of the Doody cast, but unlike most of the paltry, painted things of that time, she was so delicate, so reserved, that it took years for

Howdy to notice her, years more for him to recognize her for the charming, perfect thing she was. But when at last the scales, the crust fell from his eyes, he found himself so in love that no thing in this world or the next would ever hold any pleasure for him without her.

The perfect sweetness of their love renders itself in my memory in a simple scene. I see the two of them on a Saturday morning, still in their pajamas, splayed before the TV, holding hands chastely and watching their favorite shows: *Brother Buzz, Crusader Rabbit, Beany and Cecil, Andy's Gang.*

Ah, but memory won't let me pass that last so breezily. There was, after all, *Andy's Gang*, and the simple, raw possibility of such a show goes a long way toward explaining the woe that is in this world. For if nothing else could convince you, *Andy's Gang* could convince you that there was evil, was malice, essential as marrow, flagrant as a footstone, and wholly without motive. So sinister was the show that Howdy often had to lead the saddened and confused Story Princess from the room, just to spare her what little he himself could see that she was spared. But Howdy was fascinated by Andy's "Mob," as he called it, fascinated by something real and yet so foreign he could hardly understand it. Officially, he thought the show was artless, and he suspected Andy Devine of being a child molester. Yet he watched it worried and rapt, seeing in it a threat to the popularity of his show, and a menace to the health of the beautiful kids who filled his Peanut Gallery. Seeing *Andy's Gang* was for Howdy the discovery of an ugliness that made his own daily beauty somehow corrupt. Or, worse yet, stupid.

"Hi-ya, kids. Hi-ya, hi-ya, hi-ya."

That was Froggie the Gremlin, how he'd welcome us to the show. A presence as dark and deep as buried children, as the base purposes of animals. But how he'd rouse 'em in the gallery! The kids would lift from their ordinary lives and begin to storm. Some of the little girls would even rise up in the air, the boys clawing at their legs, panties, buttocks. And then Andy himself, every week's witting victim, would come on stage and sit in his chair— avuncular, doomed. At a certain point in every program he and Froggie would have a talk with the kids about things like "daily duties."

"Ya know, kids," Andy would say, his voice broken, whiny, bathetic, "When it's time to go to bed at night, help your parents out. Put your toys away, put on your pajamas, and . . . "

"AND THROW YOURSELVES DOWN THE STAIRS."

". . . and throw yourselves down the stairs. Wait a minute, that's not what I mean! Now, Froggy, cut that out!"

Kids: "Ahhh, haaa, haaa, haaa." A little eight-year-old girl had quietly removed her panties altogether.

"Where was I. Oh yes, put on your pajamas, go into the bathroom and clean yourself up. Don't make your parents nag. Get a nice warm washcloth and clean your face. Take a toothbrush and the toothpaste and . . ."

"SMEAR IT ON THE TOILET SEAT."

". . . and smear it on the toilet seat. Ah, no, now doggone it, Froggie, not one more time."

Kids: "Ahhh, haaa, haaaa, haaaa." Now she took the hand of the little boy beside her and brought it up beneath her charming pleated skirt.

"Plunk your magic twanger, Froggie. Go away."

"AND PISS ON THE FLOOR, KIDS. PISS ON THE FLOOR."

"Froggie!"

Poof!

Now even Andy laughed, as if laughing and having a seizure, grand mal, were the same thing.

When this episode was over, Howdy's mouth hung open, his face was gray in the thin light of the television. He raised his hand to his face and felt there the rigid contours.

* * *

But not even here, in this tale to end all tales, should it seem that Howdy's life (or for that matter our own dismal, discredited lives) was one long horror. How could he have lived as long as he did, how could his show have prospered over thirteen years, how could he have so cozened fate to allow him his Story Princess, if life were but an affliction? I can give you an example of the happiness he sometimes found. For there were days when Howdy's commitment to his art, his devotion to his own ideas of puppet beauty and life, were pleasant to the point of ecstatic, were what any of us bother to breathe for.

For instance, there was once an afternoon in the studio at NBC which we spent filming many segments. Well, we'd been there for hours, we'd done some damned good work, some fine work. The Peanut Gallery, those wonderful kids, had been patient and enthusiastic and happy. We were done for the day, we were tired, and yet there was that clarity, that elation, that energy we could hardly stand to part with. When, after all, might we again come together in such joy? So, Buffalo Bob took out his harmonica and pulled up a stool and started laying down this happy foot-stomping line. Before you knew it, Clarabell Hornblow had picked up the rhythm and Doctor Sing-a-Song had joined in with that perfect tenor of his. Soon, what the heck, there we all were, the flubadub, and Dilly Dally, old Sandy McTavish, Ugly Sam, Phineas T. Bluster and even Tim Tremble, dancing and holding hands. Then Howdy himself went into the gallery and started scooping the children up in great armfuls of hugging flesh. Those kids! And soon we were in a fine unbroken circle, laughing, falling, hurtling through the studio as though through all time and space. Howdy's head was thrown back, his arms and legs spun about the pins in his joints, he opened his eyes, the ceiling vanished, the gauzy stars spread like a blanket . . . .

* * *

As you know, I am a simple toymaker. And in my time I have made many puppets both for the Doody people and others. But there is no doubt that the peculiar puppet I carved in the summer of 1960 was the most momentous of them all. I discovered, in going through a pile of scrap, a block of wood I hadn't noticed before. How I had missed it I don't know. For it was a stunning piece, one of those that virtually speaks to the puppet-maker, that cries out, "I am here! Find me!" It was a handsome piece of wood in the ordinary sense—a thick, dark walnut. But it had an extraordinary beauty—perhaps I mean an unworldliness—that attracted me. Across its upper quarter, just where I knew I would have to cut his face, ran a dark flaw, almost maroon, a burl, a moan, a black snake.

I fell to work with my knife and tools, and soon had carved the hair, the top of the head, and then the eyes. But no sooner had I smoothed the little bubbles of light than this gruesome doll began to move them and stare at me. Practically the whole length of this block was bark that clung like a reptile's scales, but I had already cut the windows to its soul and what I saw there made me afraid.

Next I made the nose, but no sooner was it made than it began to grow. It grew and grew. I cut at it with my knife, I broke it with my hands, I bit at it with my teeth, but the more I fought against it, the longer it became, the more assertive. So I let it be and began the mouth. But the mouth was hardly half done when it began to tremble, the lips swelling like buds.

Then, arrogant, drunken, this half-made boy began to mock me. "Old fool! Old toymaker! Hurry up. I have business to attend to."

As I worked, it made faces. The great dark flaw, the scar that cut diagonally across its face, writhed, making his face that of a grizzly, groundling, great auk, grayling, hurdy-gurdy, hermaphrodite, Hecate, and even Herbert Hoover. I pretended not to notice and went on with my efforts. Soon the chin, the neck, the shoulders, body, arms and hands appeared. Finally, the legs and feet were done. Then he leaped from my work bench, landed unbelievably on both feet, put his arms akimbo and announced, "I am Howdy Doody."

"You are not Howdy Doody," I replied.

"I AM HOWDY DOODY." And off he ran, out the door, down the street. I collapsed to the floor, shaken, humiliated and ashamed.

Hours, days, perhaps a lifetime later, I was awakened by the telephone. It was Martin Stone, producer of the Howdy Doody Show. "Doc," he said, "Have you seen Howdy?"

"No," I said, afraid of what would follow.

"But you've heard what happened at the studio?"

"No."

"He came in today and tore up the set. Then he locked himself in Princess Summer-Fall-Winter-Spring's dressing room and beat her up pretty good. She still won't talk about it. What the hell is going on?"

"I really don't know," I lied. God, how afraid I was of the truth, of the implications for myself.

Then began that awful prelude. This gross caricature, this seem-alike, tried to take the place of Howdy Doody.

And he actually had people fooled. You had to look closely at the Mortimer Snerdish quality, a sort of cruel stupidity, in his eyes, the trembling sneer in his lips. How he strutted about, laughing maliciously, asking people to do the ugliest things, threatening them if they hesitated. But, of course, the big question was . . . where was Howdy, our Howdy? I mean, Howdy-himself?

For weeks and months this went on. If I hadn't known better, I too would have supposed that Howdy had simply undergone some monstrous change. But there was always that mark—the purplish scar, the moan, the snake—that cleft his face like an axe stroke.

Don't ask what took me so long to act on what I understood of this deceit. If it helps any, I will simply confess that I am guilty. Guilty, guilty. Before and after. Guilty of a monstrous creation, guilty of shameful tolerance. Sure, there were extenuating reasons for my indecision, although they seem even to me woefully lame. There were, as a matter of fact, two enormous dolls, thugs, Frankensteins, assigned by Doody-the-hideous to follow me, to see that I caused no trouble. There was also a strange warp, the kind often found in dreams, in which one means to act but just doesn't ever quite get around to it until the last shocking moment when it is clear that the world is about to collapse. What did finally move me would have moved anyone.

Of course I was aware, as everyone was aware, that the saddest aspect of this very sad situation was the effect it had on our own Story Princess. She was heartbroken by the apparent change in Howdy. It was all she could do to force herself through the show. She cried often, her memory slipped, she complained of the cold, she seemed out of touch. And it was rumored that Howdy misused her. It was said that there would be no pleasant discoveries on their wedding night. It was said that disreputable sorts, people outside of the Doody circle, pimpish plowboys, men more eager for corruption than Pinocchio's Lampwick, visited them at all hours of the night. There was even a rumor that a sudden "vacation" taken by the two was in fact a visit to an out-of-state abortion clinic.

But none of this did I allow myself to understand, until one day as I passed Howdy's dressing room I saw that the door was part open. I will not try to tell you that "courage" made me enter. I am not such a hypocrite. Let's just say that I entered. What I saw there was terrible: a woman, a small woman, nude, chained by a dog's collar to a bed. On her face she wore a mask, simple and plastic, of the ever-cheerful Bugs Bunny. When I walked to the figure and removed the mask, I found that beneath it was the Story Princess. She was not dead, but there was in her eyes no sign of life.

The bruised, bitten, brutalized body of the Princess which the very hideous soul of irony had placed beneath the Bunny mask had at last made finding the real Howdy important to me. It was easy to find him. He was at his own little apartment and had been the whole time. He was alive, but I won't say he was well. I had to force open the front door. When I walked in the living room, I saw him in the opposite corner, broken. It was a sad thing to see his arms and legs collapsed grotesquely this way and that. Already he was layered with dust, cobwebs, brittle roach bodies. He really did look like some doll that had finally bored a child and now paid a doll's price, neglect and disintegration.

I went to him and began to take his pulse, but instantly the little body whispered to me. "Doc, Doc," he said, "Is it still there? Look at my left arm." I looked and saw there something I can hardly describe. On his forearm was a pale bubble of skin which, when I looked closer, I saw to be more like a flexible scab or crust. And then looking even closer, I saw two eyes, the protruding snout, the darting tongue of something like a tiny, squat crocodile. This thing lived on his arm!

"Doc, take it off. Pull the son of a bitch off."

The beast seemed to sense it was in some danger. It had withdrawn entirely within its bubble. I felt for its tail and pulled, slowly ripping it through the skin. Then I held it in my fingers where it dangled impotent and vicious. I found a jar and dropped it inside. Closed the lid down good and tight. I hid it on the kitchen shelf, back among the pickles, ketchup and jars of Best Food mayonnaise. But I can hear it to this day moving against the glass, lifting itself and falling against the sheer walls.

Once this creature had been removed, it was not long until Howdy began to stir. I explained what had happened, that an awful homunculus, dybbuk, satan-spawn, changeling, had taken his place and was, it seemed to me, in something like the process of destroying the world. He replied that he understood and feared as much. He said it was his hungry brother, Double Doody.

He said there wasn't a moment to lose.

* * *

We caught a taxi outside of Howdy's apartment and told the driver to hurry to the NBC studios. As we drove, Howdy provided me with what he understood of this situation. Some months before he had been attacked in his own apartment late at night by this perplexing puppet who claimed that he was the real Howdy Doody and that he (Howdy-Howdy) was an impostor who had unjustly enjoyed his (Double Howdy's) success, and that matters would be set straight now. Howdy was then disabled in the mad, terrifying manner I have already described: The incapacitating leech, the very toad of the unconscious, was attached to his arm. From that time, Double Doody returned only to acquaint Howdy with his most recent outrage.

"I know all that he has done with my sweet Story Princess," Howdy acknowledged.

Here, he could not take it. His head dropped and he began to cry. For the first time I felt sorry for the little face, frozen by craft into the brightest smile. The tears ripped along the slope of his grin.

But because Howdy was brave, he didn't indulge in this suffering for long. Suddenly he lifted himself and smashed his forearm against the window that separated us from the driver. "A bloody curse on your children if you're not faster, driver." He turned to me. "But there's worse to come, Doc. Today he plans to make the children mad, ruin the Princess, and end our show forever. Unless we can get there to stop him."

We arrived at the studio and Howdy jumped from the car and sprinted across the street, myself not far behind. At the set, Howdy was stopped by a security man.

"Not so fast, mister, the Howdy Doody Show is on the air."

"Why you fool, you blockhead, *I'm* Howdy Doody."

The perfunctory, galling man stared in bewilderment. Then with a roar of impatience Howdy knocked him aside and broke through the studio door. And there it was, the last installment:

In the Peanut Gallery, the children simmered, rising and sitting, rising and sitting, their eyes fixed on an atrocity. On the stage Double Doody romped and bucked astride the Story Princess, a nifty stetson hat in his hand, his hand high over head. "EEE-HAH, call me Howdy! Call me Pecos Bill! Give me land, lots of land, under starry skies above! But don't make me stop!" His creaseless, dovetailed buttocks rose and fell mechanically, his hips rolling on pins.

Howdy leaped across the room, nothing but rage, grabbed devil-Doody from behind, spun him and with one immense, poetic, Jim-dandy of a roundhouse, punched him right on the jaw. The gallery, the crew, everybody leaped to their feet, cheering, glad at last. Howdy lifted the fallen form of the Story Princess and took her in his arms. The audience began to weep in happiness. She recognized her true lover and fell onto his chest.

But my gaze was elsewhere. The Other Doody was, after all, my creation, and I knew his strengths and weaknesses better than anyone else. I saw for one thing that the force of Howdy's punch had caused the seam in Double Doody's face to split. His head now hung together only at the neck and his eyes stared singly from two sides, like a hammerhead shark's. Dead, you say? You forget, he was a puppet. What was it to him if his head forked at the neck? So, as Howdy comforted the Princess, Double pulled from some fathomless resource a dirk. He had one intent.

You know how, in the old Saturday afternoon cowboy movies, at the moment where the bad guy was about to shoot our hero—Gene Autry, Roy Rogers, Hopalong, the Lone Ranger—in the back, the sidekick would yell, "Watch out, Roy!" and Roy'd turn, shooting precisely from the hip? Needless to say, this was the moment at which Howdy needed the fortunate warning. But who was there to shout?

It was Double's turn to spin Howdy. He forced the dagger squarely into the gut. When he removed it, fuzzy kapok clung to the blade. For a moment it seemed funny. It was so much what you don't expect in a stabbing. But it was only seconds before we realized that this wound was like puncturing the bag of the world. A bubble in which we had long found our comfort had been perforated. A terrible, sucking force ripped the smiles from our faces.

In the Peanut Gallery the children boiled.

Critical Theory

I had promised myself when still a very young man that I would never read Hegel. It was largely a matter of: Thus far but no more! A lively filament, aglow in my every cell, urged "There must be pleasure." To be sure, that principle had been long ago cozened, compromised, led to declare with conviction, "This Heidegger, he's a lot of fun." So, Hegel was the last antagonist of an already abandoned identity. In refusing him I clung to a history of myself that I had earlier denied. What resistance endured lived in a rebuslike equation; the tidy knot of his name, Hegel, referred to the crimp in an anus. Reading him would thus be like interpreting an incision in the intestines, the eschatology of a scatology, a shiterie. This powerful stupidity was sufficient for years.

Nonetheless, I begin this story by describing a moment when, lost in the midst of my thirty-third year, there I was, pulled off to the side of the road, my emergency flashers twitching in the daylight, reading Hegel's *The Phenomenology of Spirit*. Once in a while a semi would burst by blowing miserable dust and flapping the pages, and I would lift myself in amazement from those difficult words and wonder, "What sad and strange necessity is it that has caught me?"

Ordinarily, I would have stayed on the road, "made time," proceeded with the conviction of a particle beam that smells ground zero. I needed to get somewhere near the Oklahoma border by evening. I'd roared past St. Louis and had found the first whipping obstinacies of the Ozarks trifling, when suddenly there it was: Need. I had to stop and read Hegel or fail to understand something crucial. So I sat on the side of U.S. 60 just beyond Winona and considered the intangibles of the Universal Subject, all the while brewing a tepid rebellion: Tomorrow the coffee would be much stronger. Tomorrow I would be nature's uncritical boy.

It was early May of 1985 and I was driving from Illinois to California to join my young daughter. My ex-wife, Grenda, and I had divorced two years before, and it had become my summer routine to make the interesting drive through the southwest to California, and thence by a variable and usually circuitous route back to the midwest where Trudy (said daughter) and I would alternately huddle and perspire through a too-short July. But this year was to be a little different. If, I was by Grenda informed, I could possibly discipline myself to arrive in Oakland no later than 5 p.m. on May 12, I could have Trudy for an additional six weeks while Grenda and her boyfriend, Thorvald, sped boats in large circles on a distant, nameless, and very absurd lake. A vacation she called it, although I was reminded by it of nothing so much in the world as Dante's little boat ride with Phlegyas in Canto VIII of *The Inferno*. "Now thou art caught, guilty soul!"

Altogether, then, I had five days to get to California, this being the eighth of May. It wasn't a lot of time, but it was manageable, even taking the southern route as I was. But it certainly wasn't so much time that I could afford to sit on the side of the road, my first day's drive only half completed, dipping a pathetic wooden ladle into work the equal of a deep-sea canyon, into which was folded the broken hulls of barges, frigates and *fin de siecle* luxury liners, caught like toys: the great philosopher of *Geist*, G. W. F. Hegel. So, the obvious question was, why was I beginning such a project now, of all times?

* * *

The second part of this story, quite apart from but similar to Curt's struggles in the American southwest, caught between Hegel and a hard place (his wife Grenda's control of his heart's joy, Trudy), is the much more than merely academic story of the so-called Frankfurt School, the creators of Critical Theory. I am particularly interested in several crucial events in the lives of Max Horkheimer and Theodor Adorno.

The Frankfurt School was founded as the Institute for Social Research in Frankfurt in 1923 during the brief ascendency, *entre le guerre*, of the Weimar Republic. The Institute was from the outset fundamentally Marxist. Among its first leaders was Max Horkheimer, who was subsequently joined by some of the Institute's best-known figures: Erich Fromm, Herbert Marcuse, Walter Benjamin and in 1938, the most gifted of their theorists, Theodor Wiesengrund- Adorno.

When Hitler rose to the chancellorship in 1933, the consequent legitimation of the Brown Shirts and their endearing notion of intellectual give-and-take forced the Institute to leave Germany. After a brief stay in Geneva, Horkheimer accepted a generous offer of support from Columbia University in New York City, there to begin the true period of exile.

The Institute's seventeen years in America were both fruitful and frustrating for its members. The experience of American culture gave them fresh insight into the nature of Authority, but their immersion within that culture also alienated them from their own language, philosophical tradition, and desired audience—all of which were simultaneously suffering from the brutal dispersions of Nazism. The Institute's only American audience was its empiricist colleagues in the social sciences, like Paul Lazarsfeld, who spent most of their energies misunderstanding the function of theory and insisting upon the importance of questionnaires.

But it is the year 1941 which is of most importance to me. For in that year Adorno and Horkheimer moved from New York to L.A. It's obscure to me why they went, what waited for them there. Of course, their subsequently lionized confrere, Herbert Marcuse, would eventually come to roost in sultry, brick-red San Diego. (I heard him, in fact, in San Francisco in 1970, following the Cambodian invasion. He was large, old, and quite

German. His talk reminded me of stories about Hegel mumbling lectures before his stupefied students. He had no charisma to take us where thought couldn't.)

All I can say with any certainty is that Horkheimer and Adorno left on the morning of September 7, 1941, carrying several valises of papers, books, and clothing down from Horkheimer's apartment on the lower west side, near the Lexington subway line, at approximately Park and 60th street. A university car, Plymouth, 1940, nearly new, waited at the curb. They had borrowed it for the trip west. It reminds me a lot of the very used car my mother bought in 1957. I think there was some sort of boat for a hood ornament. It was probably supposed to be the Mayflower, but to European expatriates it was surely only metonymic of their status as refugees. I loved the chrome on the dashboard, the velvety, worn feel of the upholstery, the plastic imitation pearl knobs, and, especially, the dusty smell of passed time. My mother was just a girl when the car was manufactured. But when I sat in that car, it was as if I sat in time's soup, and I swear the air was so thick I could taste her death.

It was a brisk morning, temperature in the 40s. Our German friends wore hats and overcoats. Horkheimer got behind the wheel.

"So, Max, you know how to drive this thing?" asked Adorno.

"I'll learn."

"And you know where in the world it is we have to go?"

"Nearly."

"So, I can sit here with my hands in my lap and be sick

to my stomach probably before we get out of town."

"Try to enjoy yourself."

"I'd feel better if it hadn't been for the dream I had last night."

"Not the dreams again, Teddie. Are you going to tell me your dreams clear across country?"

"Sometimes my dreams are pure meshugana. But this dream was evil and true."

"Okay," turning to his friend, pretending exasperation, "I'm sure I'll have to hear this one eventually, so I may as well get it over with. Tell me the dream."

"This one was not so stupid as the one with the parrots and the board games. I dreamed that three Gestapo came here to America for me. They had on the long leather coats and fedoras. They walked toward me and I tried to hide behind my hands, like you see people do in these movies. But just as they reached me, they turned into cardboard cutouts, like props, pretend Gestapo. And out from behind them came three young women, beautiful like young starlets, golden hair, laughing. They came over and wrapped their arms around me so that I could not escape and I could not breathe. It was horrible."

Just then Max Horkheimer let out the clutch, far too quickly. The car convulsed and stopped dead.

* * *

"Did you see an armadillo? Did you think carefully through the question armadillos pose for us all?"

Well, I was just east of Oklahoma City when I saw my first, toppled over at the side of the road, victim of a Ford

Bronco. Of course, I pulled over to have a closer look, and what I saw led me on a wild series of speculations on the nature of difference. For there is nothing in the world as Otherly as an armadillo.

To begin with, the face of an armadillo is like that of an astonished and anorexic pig. You can see from that pinched expression that no armadillo has ever been clever. He has the eyes of a habitual user of hashish, the hypersensitive ears of one caught in a terror that is daily and in excess of any real need. There is also a general downward tendency in the neck that bespeaks eons of groveling, playing the toady. And while there is a superficial competence about the scaly armature, there is, unlike a fish, nothing brilliant about it. One grants, though, that the armadillo, through no virtue of his own, is generally well conceived. He certainly does a "job of work." But there is something contemptible about its tail, which it drags about officiously, as if it were something really considerable, like the tail of a stegosaurus. Here, though, the puny gesture only grates. Finally, the tiny feet, which in another context might seem charmingly dainty, here create such a disgust, seem so fulsome, so utterly without grace, so revolting and nauseating that, instinctively, one's hand quivers for a carbine. And it seems that, however important nature's delicate economy, one could not come across enough of the hollow little corpses, brittle as bug husks. Let's litter the desert with them and be done with it.

Later, I found myself trying to balance the bizarre creature on its quite dead little legs, encouraging it to walk. What in the world was I doing? Here I was on a trip of great and now greater urgency and I had once again pulled off to the side of the highway, this time to play with road-kill. I tried to blame it on Hegel. He'd never seen an armadillo, even in the Black Forest. Sure, he was in no hurry. Good time Charlie Hegel. He'd want to stop in Amarillo, too, and see if he could eat the 72 oz. steak we'd been reading about on billboards. "Your meal is free if you eat it all!" If he dawdled over a liqueur afterwards, he could talk about armadillos while drinking amaretto in Amarillo. In the meantime, the sun was setting.

The next day, the 10th, I decided to take a detour off old route 66, up to Stillwater there to visit an old lover, Doree. I understood her to be generally married now, but being in her state led me to recall the acid tang of her sweat and, like a Siren, the particular sound of her peculiar moan. So I phoned ahead and made plans to stay for dinner.

Doree and her husband lived in a condo on the west side of town. It was a re-vision of a sort of Renaissance chalet, with Queen Anne towers, Beaux Arts details and infrequent lines reminiscent of Bauhaus. Unhappily, the effect was completely undermined by bright orange dumpsters set in front of each unit, as if, without their weight, the whole complex would flip over backwards.

Doree looked good. She'd apparently quit graduate school in her eighth year of study. Following her marriage, the call of the "real world," she explained, had become overwhelming. She had married an Iranian named Pez. He looked a hell of a lot like Bani-Sadr to me and for one terrifying moment I thought I understood what was really going on, that Doree was now part of the Iranian government in exile, that she and her husband spent every day awaiting the inevitable death of Khomeini and the commencement of their own real work.

Pez prepared dinner. "This is an authentic Persian meal," he explained, "although not all of the native ingredients were available to me." As far as I could tell, the food was simply hamburger in which were raisins bloated and distended with grease, a can of spinach and slices of Wonder Bread for delivering the delicacy to our mouths.

Later that evening Pez got drunk on cooking sherry and collapsed under the table. Doree and I got in her car and drove to Lake McMurtry to split a quart of beer and listen to Steely Dan on the tape deck. "You should know by now that it's just a spasm, Babylon sister!"

Doree jerked the top off a clear quart of Millers and took a swallow. Handing the bottle to me she asked, "How's it going?"

"I'm fine," I said.

"I can't believe you drove all the way up here, hours out of your way, just to see if you and I would still screw if we were given the chance."

I couldn't recall that Doree was so brutal. I tried to whine my way out of it. "I'm not doing very well."

"Sure. You're divorced, you miss your daughter, you flounder around, self-conscious as a fish. But doesn't it bother you that I'm married now? 'Course, it didn't bother me that you were married. Before. You probably wrote Pez off as pure spaz. Am I right? And now if I were to take off my blouse, boy, we're gone god knows where."

We sat in the car and drank the beer, kissed a few times but when it counted neither of us knew where to summon desire that wasn't qualified by one irony or another. At one point I did unbutton her blouse and said something about how she was still pretty, but we both felt sort of dumb about it so she buttoned herself back up and drove us home. Last thing, she sat me down on the sofa with a blanket and a pillow and gave me a kiss on the cheek.

Of course, I couldn't sleep. Trudy appeared before me when I shut my eyes, a tiny ghost of summers future, wondering where her Daddy was and would he be late? I ran from Doree's condo, got in my car and started driving, but I hadn't gotten half way back to the interstate before I pulled off into a field of maize and fell asleep. It was nearly noon the next day before I woke, the steering wheel cutting into my chin, bleary and baking in the Oklahoma sun.

* * *

While there was little of Curt's urgency about the transcontinental movement of our critical theorists, there was all of their own habitual economy of means. They were free to dawdle if they liked, but they didn't know how. Consequently, when they awoke on their second morning, lifted their heads from the clean, cool, sturdy pillows that America's motels were justly famous for at that time, they had already proceeded clear across Pennsylvania, to Wheeling, in fact, and were now poised at the rim of the Appalachians' last hillock, ready to sled onto the great brown shelf that is the U.S. from Cleveland to Denver. But first there was breakfast at Dottie's Cafe, where the coffee was still a dime and a short stack of flapjacks (with real Wisconsin butter, Vermont maple syrup) was fifty cents.

Already, Horkheimer and Adorno had begun to feel that dissonance (for Teddy not to be confused with an embraceable *atonality*, but rather more like impending *damage*) of the sameness of American difference. Bundled into their Plymouth, as nervous as fugitives from the Mann Act, to them the American scene was completely alien. But what was immediately clear was that within this strangeness was a curious redundancy: Bloomingtons were compounded (Ind., Ill., Minn.) like a ludicrous geographic stutter. Every little town's main street was called Main Street.

So as they sat at Dottie's counter, eating and really rather liking their pancakes, they tried to figure how America fit, how the guy with the spatula, the little navy cap, and the sour puss was part of the Class Subject. He looked like a prole, but what was in his head? A commitment to Westinghouse, Philco, and Chrysler? It was all immediately discouraging. For leftist intellectuals, Jewish aliens, the great hubbub in Europe, the war against Fascism, was beginning to look like a double bind.

When they got back to their car, the coffee making

them buzz like fluorescent lights, Max said, "The—what did fair Dottie call them? griddle cakes?—were good, but too heavy for breakfast. Don't you think?"

"Yes, my stomach is sick. Drive slowly."

* * *

By the afternoon of the 11th, disgust, guilt and dread had finally overwhelmed my indulgent toying with self-destruction. I was afraid. If I were late, would Trudy feel abandoned? Would Grenda take her on vacation? Would I see my daughter at all that summer? Would Thorvald know some smart-ass lawyer who could demonstrate to a shocked and appalled magistrate that I was in my essence a present danger, a threat to Trudy's well-being?

It is enough to say, foot was applied to accelerator. New Mexico was a glimmering specter in my rearview mirror. I slept that night just short of Flagstaff and was up at dawn on the twelfth. But I wasn't much beyond Needles, had only just begun to penetrate the northern Mojave, beyond which stretched the San Joaquin Valley, vast as Kafka's China, when I realized that no matter how I manipulated speed and distance I would reach Oakland by nightfall at best. My 85 and 90 m.p.h. was "fast," but I felt as impotent as a centipede who, for all his hundred legs, could never, never make it across a street.

Worse yet, I wasn't really going to Oakland. My daughter didn't live in Oakland, my wife wouldn't live in Oakland, there being still no there there. In reality, I needed to be at 703 Muy Buena Vista Drive in San

Rafael. Which meant I had to take the Nimitz, playing Ben Hur with the trucks, then up past Berkeley, before at last being run off the freeway down into that putrescent bayside pox-box (am I getting carried away?) called Richmond. And all for the indescribable privilege of driving across the Richmond-San Rafael bridge.

Yes, I'm being unreasonable, but it was a very irritating drive. Other people kept using the streets, getting their cars in front of me. It was eight-thirty.

When I pulled up to the house it was almost nine. I was in that awful condition where you know something horrible can happen, but the terms of that something-horrible are so open-ended that you have no idea what to prepare for. There were no cars out front. The only light was from the interior, but it was enough to show, darkly silhouetted, a little figure perched on the porch steps. It was my little sweetie!

"Trudy!"

"Daddy!"

We ran to each other, hugged, and at that moment I realized something was wrong. Trudy seemed covered with a thick layer of mud. I hardly recognized her.

"How in the world did you get so filthy?" I asked.

"I don't know, Daddy."

I wiped at her with some kleenex, but it wouldn't come off. She wasn't muddy; she seemed made of mud.

"Yuck, honey. How did you get like this?"

"I was fine until Mommy left."

"You mean your mother's not here?" This was shocking.

"Yes. She left this afternoon. She said to sit on the porch and you'd come in a few minutes. I'm hungry. Can we go to McDonalds?"

Trudy's mother, my Grenda, would not leave her only child sitting alone on a porch for a minute, let alone hours. For the first time I was suspicious. Perhaps she was able to leave this child sitting because this child wasn't our child at all. I looked at her and wondered: changeling? ringer? It was as if my wife had left a tar baby for me to vacation with.

I wouldn't have been surprised if this were just one of Grenda's tricks on me. For there were other times when she, then wife, had thrown herself most imaginatively into the creation of numbing uncertainties. For instance, I recall one morning sitting at the breakfast table, regarding my own slick features in the toaster, when Grenda walked in. I looked up to say hello, but said nothing because she had cinched her nice soft house dress with a new belt. It was an ordinary gold chain, but dangling weighty at the ends, like a couple of bola balls, were two human eyes.

"Morning, sweetheart," Grenda said.

I said nothing. She took some dishes to the sink and turned. "Curtis! What's the matter? You don't say good morning to me?"

I stared at her waist. She looked down. "What is it? Is it one of those spiders again, on my dress?"

"Grenda," I said, "Whose eyes are those?"

A worried, no, frightened, no, beleaguered and despondent, yes, look came to my Grenda's face. Gently lifting each of the eyes, she walked over to me, my sanity cupped in her hands like testicles.

"Curtis, sweetheart, tell me, what are these?" Sure enough, they weren't human eyes at all. They were porcelain eggs, a dancing pig with a hat and cane painted on each. I felt a little sick.

"Darling, I wish you'd stop seeing things. It scares me."

Stop seeing things! Well, what am I supposed to do with my eyes?

Trudy took me from these recollections by whining about a Ronald's Happy Meal in a way only my one and true Trudy could. I couldn't deny her.

"Trudy," I said, taking her slightly mealy hand, "I love you. But what has happened?"

She was getting frightened. She began to cry, tears popping out like beguiling suds. "I don't know, Daddy."

We went to my car and I got an old blanket out to cover the front seat. "Now be careful when you get in. I don't want dirt all over the upholstery. And watch your shoes. That green stuff on your heel is the worst." Of course, no matter how much I urged or how hard she tried, the filth spread: a knee on the dash, a chocolate smudge of goo on a seat. Did I deserve to be thrown so quickly into the pettiest slough of fatherhood? Repeat after me, "Your child is more important than your possessions. Your child . . ."

I started the car and as we drove away from her home

I turned to her and said, "I don't know what we're going to do about this."

That made Trudy even more frightened. "Well, Daddy, you know what Marx said: 'You have to think the world by a different thought.' Can't I just be part of that different thought?"

Boy, that really burned me. Once again I was sure I was being had. "I suppose your mother told you to say that," I said.

* * *

The reason Horkheimer and Adorno made such good time traveling across country was that it was a largely incorporeal experience for them. They were not just friends, they were kindred spirits. They shared each other's ideas to a near-religious degree. As they drove, their talk about theory utterly absorbed them both. But look out the window there: gulches, beaten windmills, punched cows, tumbled weeds. They're in Texas already! And I think they forgot to eat lunch!

Adorno had been obsessing about their American colleague Paul Lazarsfeld ever since Tulsa. What really bothered Adorno about Lazarsfeld was that his empiricism, his "science," was based upon "questionnaires," whatever they were worth.

"And how, Max, am I supposed to test my insights about reification, commodity fetishism and false consciousness through surveys addressed to victims?"

"You can't."

"That's right! And these social scientists are always

so sober about their 'research instruments.' They always begin:

Survey

Most items can be answered by placing a check (✓) mark in the blank box ( ). Please respond appropriately.

"Would it be appropriate if I left half a tuna sandwich and a glass of milk in the box?" Adorno asked, whooping at his joke.

"Ha, ha, Teddie."

Adorno snorted, laughed, began to wheeze.

"I hate the objectivity of science, Max. Never forget that. It's as fraudulent as a novelist's omniscient narrator. By the way, in your opinion, who is this 'omniscient' 'third person'? How much does he really know? Does he know when we are sleeping or awake? Does he know when we've been good or bad? Respond in the space provided, Max."

Adorno's gleeful satire concluded when, only about ten miles outside of Amarillo, the Plymouth ran out of gas, thus rebutting, with that brutality typical of American automobiles, the relevance of theory.

"This is a fine mess," said Adorno. "Now what do we do?"

"It's very simple, Teddie. We start walking toward town. Maybe someone will pick us up."

Once they started walking, they found they liked it. They enjoyed being suddenly actually in the environment. They liked the rocks, they liked the grass, they liked the 'hoppers buzzing about them.

About a mile into their trek, something very strange happened. A most peculiar animal came out of the brush on one side of the road and sprinted across to the brush on the other side.

"My God! What is that thing?"

"It is the American tank-pig!"

Adorno took off after the weird animal—with evident admiration, although we know not what intent—kicking up little blizzards of dust as he ran by a creosote bush.

Max was left behind, screaming, "Teddie, you crazy, where are you going? Think what other monsters you might find out there. Flying snakes, enormous crawling desert fish, who knows? I don't like to think about it! Come back!"

* * *

From any perspective, the problem Trudy and I shared was enormous. It was no aberration, no mix-up, no oversight, no simple misunderstanding, no cross-purposed supposing. I couldn't "clear it up" with a phone call.

Of course, some of you may wonder why I didn't simply haul my smudge of an offspring over to Grenda and demand an explanation. Perhaps, indeed, a snow-white Trudy-double would have peeked from behind Grenda's skirt, amazed to see, at my side, what familiar monsters the earth breeds. But, friendly though that idea may be, it is delusive. My situation was my situation. It had always been my situation. I would even claim that it is every parent's situation, once one probes beneath Dick and Judy's well-scrubbed epiderm and finds there the essential murk.

I tried very hard to think through our problem in a way that seemed happy. Poor Trudy certainly worked at it. She tried to eliminate the negative: she became quite good at not rubbing up filthily against things; she managed by repeated shampooing to get something with a family resemblance to hair on top of her head. But in general the best she could achieve was a sort of messy inbetween, nothing close to the sugar, spice and everything nice one hopes for in a daughter.

So my puzzle became, quite quickly and quite logically, how to alter what I desired in her. What a task! Every night when I bent to kiss her I was confronted with it. Should I think of her as a frog princess? As Beauty's beast? But neither of these possibilities really corroborated her muddiness-in- itself, and both required from me the virtue of self-abasement that I did not possess. How could I make myself want Trudy's beastliness for its own sake? If she was the daughter of the Creature from the Black Lagoon, then I had to become the Creature from the Black Lagoon! It was that simple.

Well, I'd like to be able to report to you how successfully I did just that. I'd like to describe for you how I now line the inside of my sports coupe with fungus. But I can't just yet, although that remains an important project I have in no way forgotten. Unfortunately, immediately upon our return to the midwest, I began teaching a seminar on the Sublime. Hegel, Kant, Schiller, Goethe:

those blokes cloaked me in gauzy raiment. I had no other choice than to postpone the rapprochement with my daughter.

Nevertheless, I think she's having a good summer. I bought her a dog—a bassett hound that delights in getting down and dirty—and now the two of them tumble in the backyard, best of chums. Harvard (that's what we call the hound, "Harvard") thinks that Trudy is a dog's dream of a human. I agree. For a while I hosed them off after they played, but I worried that it was Trudy essentially that puddled at my feet.

Soon, it's true, she will return to her mother, and I will have done nothing to free either of us from the ideas that keep us apart. But at least I can say that I live consciously at the cusp of my contradictions. I have maintained the sanity of difference. *This* is my child. *These* are our problems. The world is not an elaborate hoax perpetrated by those who do not love us. Therefore, we may be happy yet. I have hope for it.

* * *

Sadly, the Frankfurt School thinkers felt largely defeated either by or during their American years. Walter Benjamin died a strange suicide on the Spanish frontier; the cloak was removed from the great Nazi secret: the camps. And then, following Hiroshima, the visage of nuclear death commanded that the future be imagined in horrible new ways, a gloomy project that we, Critical Theory's heirs, continue to this day. These events were of such magnitude as to modify and in some ways render obsolete the Marxism they had brought with them from Frankfurt.

In 1949, Horkheimer and Adorno returned to Germany to rebuild the Institute in Frankfurt, only blocks from the ruins of their original office. The two old friends continued to work closely together, but for the first time in their careers important kinds of differences began to appear, differences that mutual affection and shared history hardly allowed to be expressed. In particular, Horkheimer began to downplay, if not outright suppress, his own earlier Marxist essays. No longer was he so willing to equate capitalism with fascism. Instead, he embraced—however awkwardly and apologetically—religion, empirical social studies, and the idea of the "healthy liberal."

Adorno, on the other hand, remained committed to the creation of aggressive, explosive ideas. But however much Adorno remained in the vanguard conceptually, by the 1960s his aggressiveness had been outstripped in praxis by the New Left. Working from pirated editions of the Frankfurt School's earliest work of the '30s, the New Leftists went on to realize Critical Theory's conceptual models with, in Adorno's words, "Molotov cocktails." Teddie then became, in the most haphazard way, the object of his own critique.

This process culminated in April 1969 when three members of a militant group attacked Adorno during a lecture by baring their breasts and pelting him with flowers. He was shocked at first, but decided that the best thing to do was simply to wait it out. This strategy proved insufficient, however, when the three women began caressing him and rubbing up against him most lasciviously. Enclosed by their unwanted fleshiness, Adorno experienced an Albigensian moment of pure disgust with the corporal, as if he'd been traduced by meat for the last time. This led to a hallucination in which he saw himself, excrement dripping from his tongue, and before him an audience, a cast of thousands, composed of every person he'd ever known or conceived of, including his father, Oskar, the wine merchant, his teacher Hans Cornelius, Lulu, Arnold Schönberg (who was trying to persuade a corpse to deliver Adorno a note which read, "You are a traitor!"), Walter Benjamin (who gestured for Teddie to come closer, but couldn't quite make himself heard), Humphrey Bogart ("I hate to play you for a patsy, kid, but . . ."), Hitler himself ("I was a naughty man!"), Danny the Red ("The victims do not matter . . ."), Gustave Mahler ("*In diesem Wetter, In diesem Brau!*"), and that ain't all. From behind three colossal curtains workers rolled refrigerators made in Albert Speer's retooled war industry, yours courtesy of the economic miracle, which lined up behind Teddie like an awkward, girlish Stonehenge. 'Twas then he realized that what had seemed a general, generous cacophony of applause was in fact the crowd's disciplined chant, ringing in the new: "Adorno is dead! Adorno is dead!"

I suppose we should all prepare for an equally noodled end and not "the distinguished thing itself." Yes, there will be important differences between our eventual defeat and Adorno's, and I suppose that it would be important and desirable if someone did a proper accounting of those differences, like a teaspoonful of the vital pap of particularity administered by mom, each to each. To see the truth of the singular dozing with little belches of contentment in the arms of the general! Clarity! Justice! Reason!

But don't count on it.

The Order of Virility

> . . . trench confessions,
> Laughter out of dead bellies.
> —Ezra Pound

"Phan-TAS-ma-goria! Meta-mor-pho-SEEZ! Come see what the gods have wrought! Come see the fierce Order of Virility! Young blood and high blood, fair cheeks, and fine bodies! Manhood: the greatest show on earth! Step right up! Ten cents please."

This is no joke, though I joke. Though I play at barker, I'm part of this sideshow. Professor Ike Schilling, my most familiar self, is himself constellated for his wickedness among these many dark stars. And not only constellated but—as I can show you—made the centerpiece, as if we were the constellation of the pig and I the apple in the pig's mouth. Conspicuously, around my neck hangs the logo of our guild, what we as a Klan have allowed carved of our flesh. It looks innocent enough: a jaunty decoration, dangling embellishment. But remove it from the neck and it is a snare for young hares. Or gripped in a fist and yanked upwards it is a halter—homey in some way, of one's own making.

And yet it has not always been so. I have not always been a member of this Order, this thumb's smudge in ink. (A stern hand grips the back of my neck. Is that you, God-the-father? Whose side are you on? He insists that I say that "not always having been a member of the Order" means only that there was a time before I was caught and known.) As recently as 1932, the hermaphrodite (whose presence on my left is manliness's lone irony) and I were free to tour the dusty back roads of Iowa, Illinois, and Indiana through towns of people stupefied by corn. How eager they were to see a man who could buckdance on a wagon tongue, who sold bottles of liver syrup with pictures of Cassandra of Crete on the label, and who allowed those most disturbed at heart to gaze by lamplight on the boy's complicated sex.

Yes, the "boy" was museum quality. He rivaled Miss Ada Scott, whose skillful handling of snakes has astonished thousands in this country; the Princess of Zirmekia; the Horned Man; the little armless wonder; the two-headed girl; old Black Simmons, who has been turning white for years; Kee Kee the hot iron performer; Jones, the glass eater; big Winnie Johnson, of 500 pounds weight; the spotted boys; the man alligator; old whistling Charley; Kuro, the Congo Giant; and the ossified man. But the boy's lure was special and deep. And while he exhibited to a man the folds and textures of his grotesque essence, I demonstrated for the client's wife the soothing subtleties of an oil, unguent, obtained of an albino ram, found only in tenebrous Irkutsk. For Professor Ike Schilling has a "freak" of his own: I was born in a desert and raised in a lion's den. My only true occupation has always been taking women from their men.

* * *

It was a Saturday when we pulled our wagon into laughable Peru, Illinois.

"Where are the Andes?" asked the boy.

"I's Andy if you's Amos," I replied.

"If you's 'andy, then nought's amiss."

"What the ladies all say!"

The townsfolk looked at us as if we were the first things to move in two weeks. When we came out of our wagon, blacked-up, Ethioped, they rose and dusted themselves off. Then the boy started in on the bones, making a fine music. "Let 'em racket, Kid!" I encouraged.

Our gentle Peruvians came up like all heart-of-the-country rubes do, sniffing, clutching together like bundles of dried sticks, kindling to our peculiar blaze. I did "Zip Coon" and "Jump Jim Crow," turned my lips into saucers, my mouth into a satchel. I rolled my eyes like an epileptic. The audience warmed to this, innocent smiles on their faces, and we began our act.

Now, the people of Illinois like nothing better than to see a half-wit get the better of an intellectual, a perfesser. So we opened the show with Professor Schilling and Mr. Stump.

Professor: Well, Mr. Stump, have you ever been to college?

Stump: Yassir, I done went to college. Took a letter up there once. Then I endorsed a chair in old Jim Nastytrick's department.

Professor: Oh, you mean endowed a chair in gymnastics?

Stump: Dat's de time. An' you kin see her to dis day. Endowed her deep and wide. Be there till she cut up for kindlin'.

I had the next line to deliver, but I looked up to catch the audience's eye. I shouldn't have. I'd seen one too many potato face that summer. They looked like lumps, turnips, tubers, behind which slumbered a certain meanness. And I thought to myself, if I steal their money and make love to their wives, it's the most lifelike thing that will happen to them this year.

The truth of the importance I played in these middlin' lives had been demonstrated often enough before. For instance, there was the time in 1929 when the hermaphrodite and I were on old route 51 outside of Louisville. It was summer and the weather was hot and sodden, so one evening after dark, as we pulled along the highway, we decided to stop and sleep in the tall, cool cat-lick grass by the side of the road. It was a good night's sleep, but we woke at the first light of day to a sound more fantastic than anything we'd ever heard. It was in part like a broken scream, in part like a tattered shout. It moaned, broke off, spit, accelerated, rose violently, dipped, collided, and then drove hatefully forward. It was the sound from which children learn of the hidden viciousness of their own parents.

The noise was coming from a beaten sort of shack just on the other side of the road. It was in fact a storefront, a grocery. Taylor's Kentucky Grocery, Vincent and Rose Taylor, Props. Needless to say, we were more than a little wary of a strange, disheveled house, hunkered in the two lights of dawn, releasing the most god-awful and scary moans, yells, and howls. For all we knew, the place was abandoned, once the scene of a murder and now the haunt of ghosts.

But when dawn changed to the good whole light of morning, the screaming stopped. Mrs. Taylor came out to open the door, sweep the porch and set out a crate of apples. The sight of such ordinary chores made us feel a little more natural, so we walked across the road.

Inside, the grocery was dim and dusty. We could feel the grittiness of the warped, worn floorboards beneath our feet. In front of us loomed the shapes of wooden shelves stacked high with canned goods. At the very back wall of the shack was the counter, but it—and the figure sitting behind it—was obscure. That was where a voice came from.

"What do y'all want?"

"We're Professor Schilling's Traveling Show," said the boy. "We're on the road and we'd like to rest here a day and night if you wouldn't mind."

"Vincent!" shrilled the voice, "We've got riffraff again. We've got drifters and moochers."

From behind the counter came the hollow, lonely bang of a man's heavy step. Then a bare overhead light was flashed on and we were able to see Vincent Taylor.

Vince, as no one in the world called him, was an ugly man. His body was large, disproportionate, angular, but plainly strong. He had one of those uniquely American paunches that told of hours spent sitting, desiring money, willing to endure any tedium or humiliation to have it. There was something evil about that roll of fat. It was made of alcohol, cigarettes, coffee, self-contempt, the mere dislike of his own children, infinite boredom, a lust as dry as the buzzing of a cicada, a loathing for the corpus, the body, the heavy limbs of his wife, and a fear of the flaccid, puttylike reflection of his own face. And there was very plainly about him the malicious avidity of the will to possess.

But most striking of all, Vincent Taylor had no left arm. He never explained to anyone why it was gone. It was simply absent, chopped off, not accounted for. Its not-presence gave to his every movement the impression of something not-human, not even animal. He seemed like something that could only contaminate.

Vincent looked down at us. "What do you want here?" The boy told him exactly the same thing he had told Rose Taylor.

But it was again Rose that answered. "Well, you two can just be off. We'll give you a couple biscuits and you can just start movin'. We don't have the time for you."

She would have gone on, but Vincent interrupted her. "They can stay."

"What!" Rose shrieked.

"They can stay."

Rose turned sharply on us looking for the cause of her

husband's generosity. "Ha, you son of a bitch," she wailed, "It's the girl, the little slut, you want the girl." Great god, she meant my boy! "You think she'll let you in 'cause you give her a potato to chew on? Not in my presence. Not in my house."

They retreated again to the rooms behind the store. "Shut it, Rose. Will you shut it."

"I'll kill you first. I'll see you in your grave. It's not bad enough that you get whores in town, or Dan Judd's young wife begging you on her knees, pullin' up her little dress to save her husband's farm. Think I don't know about that? And Mrs. Judd come up lame for a week from the awfulness of it. But this is too much. Not this hussy. Not in my own house."

"You'd better shut it, Rose, or I'll tear out that black tongue of yours."

"Cripple. Killer. Fiend."

* * *

Rose Taylor was right. Vincent's only purpose in allowing us to stay was his determination to have the boy, somewhere, in a bed if possible, slipping in the tall wet grass if need be, scrambling and scraping on the rough grocery floor if nowhere else. Of course, he worried about how his wife might try to stop him, but he figured he had thirst and strength enough to account for her as well. Maybe he'd give her a banging first. Beat her like an old pot and leave her unconscious with the surprise and force of it. Then make his intentions known to the boy. To me I suppose he gave no more consideration than he would a mosquito that could do nothing worse than nest on his bloody thigh.

Well, that very afternoon Vincent sat down to the concentrated drinking of gin. At midnight he could still be heard out in the yard, the gin splashing and gullying out of its jar into his mouth. That's when we decided to have our bit of fun and profit.

I had the boy saunter out into the yard, past Taylor, the stars spangling gaudily overhead, crass as sequins. "Evenin', Mr. Taylor," he said, sweet as you please. "I'll be retirin' now. See you in the mawnin'." A line right out of "The Atlanta Belle"! Up he climbs into the wagon and turns the lantern on low. And old Taylor, he's so stunned with booze and desire he can't say a word. But he lurches up and drops his mason jar—half-full of kerosene, or scalp tonic, or whatever in hell he chased his gin with. Then with an uneven stagger he followed the boy to our wagon.

There was something emblematic about that scene. For there were two lurid silhouettes: one, the womanish boy moving with those disturbing gestures behind the canvas of our wagon; two, the essence of virility, Vincent Taylor, struggling toward the boy—enraptured, emboldened—his figure canting weirdly away from his missing limb.

Of course, a certain sap flowed in me as well. I knew where Mrs. Taylor slept, and I knew how to punctuate her dreams in a way that would cure all her ills, " 'cause they call me Doctor Brown, they call me that naughty name." And even though I had no desire for her, and certainly no fondness, I knew my duty. You can ask any woman in your neighborhood.

But first I checked on Taylor and made sure he was diverted. I went to the wagon and looked inside. The boy was bare to the waist, a thin sheet covering his groin. Taylor was crouched above the boy's cot as over an infant's crib. His face twitched and jerked like that of a child about to cry and he made a whimpering sound, his bluish lips protruding as though he were blowing on hot soup. This was clearly a moment he wouldn't abandon for a while.

So I strolled back to the grocery, whistling an old darkie refrain. First, I went to the cash register and gently lightened its burden. Zippideedoodah! Then I made my midnight creep to the bed of Rose Taylor. Holding a fistful of dollars on either side of her head, I paid yet another small installment on mankind's collective debt.

At just precisely that moment, I heard a predictable scream from the yard. I quickly pulled on my trousers and ran out to the wagon, to make sure the boy was safe. But there was no reason to worry. In his own shocking way, he could take care of himself. He reclined casually, resting on an elbow, now completely undraped. Over him was gaping Vince, his gaze frozen on the boy's knotty groin. It was as if he'd found the stoney face of the Medusa in the youngster's crotch. It was a moment upon which Professor Schilling could have reflected with some profit, no doubt. But there's no time for contemplation, the complicated working out of Ought, in this life where Will is boss. So instead I maneuvered Vincent toward the rear of our wagon and gave him a gentle nudge, my shoulder's modest proposal, which sent him crashing to the ground. He lay there stiff, with an arm missing, looking like a broken piece of Attic statuary.

* * *

What I have neglected to mention, what I have conspicuously omitted from my tale to this point, is the fact—however unlikely you might think it, however unpredictable given other claims about my life's purpose—that I was ultimately one of love's great dupes. I could behave towards women like one of God's precise instruments of mischief and injury because I didn't care about them and didn't need them. I had a role to play, that's all. Back door man. Eat more chicken any man ever seen. All that. But, you've probably already guessed it, the boy, yes, the boy I loved. Purely. Endlessly. It was Petrarch and Laura with us. Why? All I can say is that there is a pocket, a pouch, in my side, with a delicate depression at the shoulder for his head, where my boy fits like truth, huddled, warm, sleeping gently, snoring softly.

All of which must make my shameless exploitation of his genital eccentricities seem grotesque and deplorable. But—listen to me!—I am neither block nor stone. I understand this irony in the very heart of me. But *you* should understand that although the boy was a resource I could not afford to ignore, there were limits to what I allowed. When the 'pokes and plowboys clustered around for a look-see, a pure and childish wonder on their faces, their hands twitching with the desire to probe the bewitching pinwheel at his groin, I stood close by with a gilt sword, the gift of an Emir who had used it to lop the offending hand from the arm of a thief.

And after all, that part of our life which was the show we could keep strictly contractual. I had no fear of it. The men kept to their place, the boy to his, I to mine. What I really feared was the killing thought that somewhere there was a lover's side more comforting than mine, to which the boy might cleave like a sleeper to his most delightful dream. Before this possibility I stood pathetic, limp, and craven.

* * *

"Will you take a bow, you damned old goat?"

The voice of the boy woke me. Our audience of delighted Peruvians applauded wildly. Even though I had been lost in dreamy recollection, I had apparently performed as credibly as our old friend Salvador, the Italian Somnambulist. So I did as I was instructed and took a deep bow for God knew what.

After we'd sold a few bottles of Dr. Sass's Pure Tonic (good for what ails you), we began to pack our things. Peru—with its majestic mountain vistas!— had been wonderful, but we had to hit Chenoa and Towanda yet that afternoon. That's when the good Reverend Tooth and Mae, the lovely Mrs. Tooth, emerged from the crowd, introduced themselves and thus changed our lives.

Reverend Tooth's type is rare in the Lord's ministry,

much more common in Mammon's. He was tall, fine looking, strong, assertive, and seemed completely at home in the physical. His wife, too, was a vivid, attractive woman about whom I will tell you more later. The point is that the Reverend approached us for a reason.

"I enjoyed your show very much, gentlemen." He rocked on his toes as he spoke, as if he had some secret and utterly enabling knowledge about which I hadn't a clue. Before he spoke again, he pursed his lips, stared at me deeply and placed an index finger to his mouth. It was a gesture that indicated a capacity and capability that depressed me completely.

"Your visit also seems to me providential," he continued. "For the church is in the middle of trying to put on a minstrel show of its own, using boys of the community who have little else to do in the summer. I thought I could handle it myself, but I've found that it's not such an easy thing. It requires a magic I know nothing about. Would you be willing to stay in our community long enough to teach our boys what you can about your performing? The church can pay you fifty dollars each for a week of work."

Well, since we wouldn't make a hundred bucks between us if we sold fifty bottles of Dr. Sass's Best every day for that week, the boy and I shared a quick wink and said, "We're at your service, Reverend Tooth."

We agreed to meet at the church hall that evening to inspect our gang of apprentices.

* * *

When we walked through the double church doors—

"Hello, bright strange future!"—we were met by a ludicrous, exciting, completely seductive scene. There they were, some fifteen boys, twelve to sixteen years in age, with that precise vulnerability of adolescence scrawled on their faces: they were not, there was no Self, they were whatever they were led to be by whatever was closest to hand. At that moment, it meant that the air was full of sticks, bats, balls, string, the fluff of a deceased kitten, eggshells, pages from Zane Grey, the funk of an earthworm, a squeeze play, jeepers, what mom will make of that stain, Tom Swift's floating island, what does it mean "frig"? Frigger? Frigate? 'Frigerator? Frig-it-me-not? a sock in the arm and a real hard sock in the arm.

When the boy, my boy, saw this scene, he rejoiced. He was surprised, he was delighted. He bounded in front of us, his arms open, and said, "My fellows! What I'll make of you!" He laughed out loud and hugged a few of the bumptious lads. Turning to the reverend, he said, "What a troupe we'll be. They'll be the greatest of Ethiopian songsters."

The Reverend Tooth was equally excited. And I saw for the first time on his face a welter of expressions all of which signaled desire. I might have been more wary, but, after all, the boy's appeal was my bread and butter. I was used to it, though I'd never be used to it.

Of course the Reverend's interest meant that while he and the boy tended to the creation of a certain manic craft in the adolescents, Mae Tooth could be left to my instruction.

* * *

During this ultimate and ultimately clarifying period of my life, in the dreamy city of Peru, I felt elevated beyond the meager possibilities of minstrelsy. I was part of the greatest show on earth—Seduction! Deceit! Irresponsible pleasure!—a two-ring circus at the least. For while I worked at the delicious Mrs. Tooth on one side of town, the reverend and my boy devoted themselves to their dark work on the other. What they quickly made of those muddled, middle-American lads! It was gradual, but finally sharp. So when Mrs. Tooth and I went over in the afternoons—strolling leisurely on the cobbled streets beneath the toxic breath of the oaks—and stood arm-in-arm at the church door, we saw that the puffy, unfirm roundness of their Huckleberry faces had been replaced by something keen, cutting, mordant, and more than a little cruel. In the place of a cheek had come a caustic, ebony plane. In the place of the innocent eyes of a mother's son had come something sightless, blank, and opulent. And all of this it had been my boy's great pleasure to bring about. He had gone among them like a demonic sculptor, a Svengali, a Professor Spalanzani, a voodoo queen. Where he touched them, they twitched and changed. They were no longer boys.

And from their mouths came correlatives: De maid ob de Hunkpuncas (she got de meat shakin' on her bones); Parson Doodlebug Doofunny, the Darkey Deacon; wrigglin' round with my jellyroll; Mammy Blossom's possum taste so fine!; the Coontown wedding; my gal's biscuits plenty big enough for me; what can be de matter wid de piccaninny?; woman get funny give her a mouth full of fist. This essential distillate, coming from the mannish boys, I called "cute." I had to laugh to see such sport.

But I wondered if Mrs. Tooth saw these changes as anything like "cute." Oh, she didn't adopt the pose of the high-toned Christian. I knew what to do with those 'marms. One night with the pinky tickling the old trap door and they thought that every day the world was becoming better and better. Unfortunately for my cause, Mae just seemed to see things clearly.

"C'mon," I coaxed, "this is fun for young and old."

She responded with a tolerant but unenthusiastic, "I'm sure it is."

And God knows what she saw in her husband's actions. He was never more than a step away while my boy worked at his gruesome beauty. The Reverend's mouth gaped, he was filled with awe, with an unspeakable admiration. His hands twitched constantly, his hams throbbing beneath his trousers. This absence of manly control, this lack of reserve and dignity, this willingness to let his desires be known, seemed to me shameful. I couldn't help but feel that next to it, even in the eyes of his own wife, I must look keen and desirable. That's what made it seem so strange to me that though we spent nearly every blessed hour of the day together, I made no progress with her. The most sensual thing I did that week was hold a tea cup daintily by its tepid and tiny porcelain ring.

Now, it should be clear that my job with women was not the world's easiest thing, pure fun though it may seem. I knew my role well enough: Candy Man, Salty Dog. But the women had a very particular function, too, in the absence of which things could get puzzleheaded. They had to be Beedle-um-bum (come and see me if you ain't had none); my little black angel (knows how to spread her wings); big fat mama, etc., etc.

Of course, I could be excused by saying that it's not so easy to make Li'l Miss Brown out of a parson's wife. But that was not it at all. Because she wasn't my first parson's wife. And my idea had ever been that, in the final account, all women kept in their heart-of-hearts similar desires and deserts. But it was so hard to convince her that she was as the others and not as she often seemed: as different from women as my boy from every other boy.

So there I remained for vast awkward afternoons reclined like an incongruous barroom nude in the uninterested parlor of Mae Tooth, hoping, cautious, still waiting for my moment, still husbanding a nasty hunger. Meanwhile, she chatted, poured beverages, presented cakes, suggested strolls in the garden, and generally made time so pleasant that I eventually felt (or I can see myself from my present place as feeling) drugged. It was like being fetched by lotus eaters or kindly Calypsoed. It was civil, it was even pleasant, but it was also madly contradictory. Not my job description at all.

On the day before we were to leave I was sitting in the lucid parlor of Mae Tooth, among her overgrown and threatening success with ferns and ivy and every vining, tendrilous thing that might leech my will or strap me to this place beyond my time. She sat opposite me discussing issues, books, names, politics—all that which no others in Peru knew of, but to which I, being traveled, could at least nod. Finally, I thought, "This is the last whimpering day. I've left my job undone, my mojo ain't workin'. It's time for the black snake moan."

So, I made a tremendous effort, lurched free of my own crusted form and made my creep. She did not seem surprised. She said, "Ah, is that what you want, Professor?"

"You bet, sweet mama!"

"That is a pity. Too bad. No thanks."

So I took her by the waist and gave her a taste of my tongue, second cousin to Little Johnny Cockaroo himself, which she accepted in her mouth with the enthusiasm she'd have given to a rancid gherkin.

I could hardly believe it. "Well, tell me, woman, don't you want a man like me?"

"Yes, no, maybe so." She almost smiled, obviously taking none of this really seriously, her plain, intelligent face making me feel almost foolish. And then she did laugh a little. Yes, she thought it was funny.

I began to back out, gather my things, feeling really nasty. "We'll see who laughs, woman," I said. "Those boys we're training will be at your window soon, just watch. And that's not all. When they're older and they've got their bag, and the real stuff in it, the reverend himself will stand 'em at the foot of your bed and up the chute they'll go."

Mae just looked at me. Oh, I was a cocksman, alright. Killer-diller.

So I did leave then, depressed, angry and confused, hardly knowing what to make of myself anymore. At least she wasn't laughing when I left. In fact, when I last looked back I could see, through a little window, that she was crying, simply. Apparently, our talk hadn't been a life-enhancing experience for her. I suppose that makes her sympathetic. I suppose a person shouldn't have to suffer for not wanting to be my genitals' fool. My only consolation was that there was still the true fire of my love for the boy. He never said things like "Yes, no, maybe so." He never smiled when I wanted the Real Thing. He knew what love was about. I decided I'd wait for him on the cot in our wagon, cool a few bottles of Dr. Sass which had been particularly aged, and then enjoy a long night of what heat was all about. We'd make the wagon bounce like the famous Phoenician Flea. A nice "So long, sucker" to Peru.

But before the boy arrived, I fell asleep. And when I awoke the next morning, I was alone. Do you know what panic is, oh my reader? Do you know what it's like to have something lodged in your heart, the size of a pea, a radioactive pippin, which is all at once the anxiety of what could be, the despair of what is, the grief of what has been? I climbed out of the wagon and ran to the church hall where I found the following: Sleeping, sprawled in all directions, were the newly savaged, those boys-next-door who had been transformed into black-faced beasties, infernal guardians, neighborly Cerberi, who plainly now slept in the way that something really evil sleeps: in the mere absence of present violence, the synapse before a bludgeoning.

I tiptoed through their bodies toward the back rooms afraid of what I would find there. I pulled back the door to the sacristy, my life ended, and so did this thumb's smudge of a tale. The giant, the lengthy, naked reverend stretched on a cot, the figure of my naked boy beside him, drawn into that gap at his side, more like a womb, the sack of a divine marsupial where he next to glowed. I walked across the room and stood over them. At the moment I reached down to take the life from them, as one would take a glistening eye from its socket, the boy awoke with a scream. He was a civet—spiney, fearful, fierce—alarmed from sleep by the smell of man. That one scream brought the unclean, undead, minstrel boys from the next room and they stormed about us and would have torn us apart—three undiscriminated Pentheuses before the Bacchae—had not the perhaps crueler hand of Providence intervened and plucked us out, ordered us eternally, as we deserved, as you can see at any time you choose, just open this book to page 150, and there we are, not even breathing heavily, looking like we have girl friends waiting off-stage who think we're keen, who think it's neat that we fellas are putting on a play, who think we look kinda scary in our makeup, but that's all right, they know what we're like inside, who'll share a coke with two straws over at Lundquist's five-and-dime, and who won't suspect that a spore drifts on the wind tonight.

Malice

Remember the heroic example that big Diamond Jim Brady set for us during the depression of the 1890s? While his faithless, fickle colleagues tossed the very finest pearls of free enterprise, of our fabulously free market before whatever snout would snort after them, he—that Diamond Jim—the only one of faith among the legions of unbelievers, spent his entire fortune buying up stock and industry that would be worse than paper within the year.

But because of the bounteous and gracious system within which he worked, in the end he had his riches returned and then some. Ultimately, though, he died. Like all of us, sad to say. But such a death. The doctor says to him, "James Brady, I'm not one of your little toadies. There ain't nothin' I need from you. Do you hear what I'm saying? I'm going to tell you the truth, son. I'm laying it on the line, calling a spade a spade, putting the crust of the bread on top, I'm forgetting the keyhole in honor of the door, and showing congress a rock."

Says Big Jim, sinking deep into a chair, "I think you better tell me what's on your mind, Doc."

"I want you to cut out the rich foods, is what. You got a spleen that's bankrupt. A liver with flow problems. Intestines with inflation. Your pancreas needs an independent overseer. The next oyster you eat will be your last. I guarantee."

So, what happens in the end? He's in his private superbly appointed train coach roaring across the nation, whipping over the belly of that great land, laying it one last time. The enormous diamond rings on his beefy hands spangle in the gloom as he slides oysters on the half-shell (eighty) into his mouth. He pauses only to squeeze on each a bit of lemon and to laugh against his outrageous destiny. If one couldn't have oysters, what was the point of being rich? It was better to die a martyr. So in that laugh, in the opulent swallowing of those oysters, was the poetry, the bitterness, the gluttony and the enormous injustice of life.

But Diamond Jim was a piker compared to Simon Fish, the Kansas Wheat King. When the dusters came through western Kansas in the spring of 1935 and lifted three hundred fifty million tons of dirt over Middle America, Simon was there. No doubt, at first, he was simply part of the problem. When he busted the sod to plant wheat, he was too stingy to allow room for fences. But when the rains didn't come, the crops failed, and all that pulverized topsoil just sat up waiting for the first sprite of wind in order to purl away. And when the big winds came, the hundred-mile-an-hour winds, they picked up Kansas and scattered it over Chicago like snow, four pounds of it for each man, woman, and child.

Now, most of Simon Fish's colleagues just gave it up, gave it all back to the Great American Desert. But not Simon. He took that dusty, droughty hole called Morton County, Kansas, bought an old oil pipeline and filled it with water, put down twenty acres of turf and built the visionary Palace Hotel. It was a beautiful place, three stories tall, painted luminous white, with arching haughty windows, and big-sky blue shutters. The roof too was shingled a showy blue. And then on the grounds he brought in, as I said, twenty acres of emerald turf, and mulberrys, oaks, walnuts, and every hardy, hybrid fruit-bearer that would take the winter. But, of course, the dust that came from the rest of Morton County would every day drift in malicious and filthy blizzards and threaten to bury the whole idea. That's why Simon Fish hired one thousand out-of-work farmers and their wives, bought a whole freight car full of dust mops and whisk brooms, and promised them a dollar a day plus a meal of beans and greenish ham (government surplus) to keep the dust off the lawn, off the house, out of the pond. Meanwhile, with a niblick and a pearly golf ball, he would chip his way around his grounds to see how well they did. Their job wasn't easy. For every bucket of dirt they dumped off the edge of the lawn, another ton or so descended. And the sight of themselves—wandering, buffeted by grime, wearing goggles and face masks—made them think of WWI battlefields, mustard gas, and the terrifying prophecy, "You will drown in your own blood!" Many of that desperate, brave, principled thousand just lost control at last and meandered off the lawn, off the priviliged premises of the Palace Hotel, into the murky oblivion of a duster, never again to be seen.

So for a good long while this gutsy endeavor fought a winless battle against the palpable, choking folly of earlier enterprises. The dust piled up, workers collapsed, Simon Fish lost dozens of golf balls, the Palace walls sootied. But in the winter when the ice storms came and sheeted the whole midwest, and temperatures declined to zero and below, stilling everything, even the malice of dust—why then the beauty of the Palace Hotel virtually screamed with purity in the dazzling winter landscape.

It was during those times that Simon Fish would look at what he had created and realize that it was good and lasting and bound to make him money, more money even than wheat, or at least more money per acre. Why, if every twenty acres of fly-away Kansas prairie had on it a Palace Hotel, or a golf course, that in itself would stop the Dust Bowl, seal it. And what a symbol of the survivability of capital, of the great truth that the free market has the know-how to solve its problems without the aid of nosey federal agencies bringing their socialist ideas to town, and with a loaf of bread and a job shoveling dirt buying up another good American working man. Those fellows could be serving breakfast in the Omaha Room, or trimming a green, or raking pure a trap of sand.

But I did not wish to wait for the elimination of dirt before I made my first grateful offering to Simon Fish ($20 a day for a luxury suite, meals, and active social calendar). In February of 1939 I took my winter vacation at the Palace Hotel. While my associates and their plumped wives sweltered in a Floridian delirium, ecstatic to be away from Hartford and insurance, I checked into the super-arctic accommodations of the Palace. While they frolicked in frothy Gulf waters and stood amazed before the bulky corpse of a barnacled whale, I played a game much like shuffleboard with a jovial Simon Fish out on the glassy surface of the Palace pond.

To be frank with you, I disdained venereal Florida, vacation mecca. And, more than that, I disdained the lives of those businessmen and their wives. I needed to be away from them because in all other seasons the men, my colleagues, prodded me—even at my own desk— with sinister erections. They would take the opportunity of a conference to ungrid the steel teeth of their zippers, unfurl themselves, and with a flourish drape their beating flesh over the arm of my chair. And in the spring, at a party in the lilied, tuliped garden of a Vice President of the Delineation and Perusal of Ledgers, inevitably a wife would insinuate her hand inside and behind my modest, casual, pleated trousers, and insert a horrible hooked thumb, all the while chatting about how well her favorite daughter with curls drew the breezy plume of smoke that emerged from the chimneys of little boxed houses in spacious somnolent lands. And I was always too horrified to protest or comment. I could only gasp with thankfulness when she withdrew her darkened thumb and, laughing, retreated across the patio. Before I knew it, before long, it was the thing to do, a pastime, and every wife had to try it at least once in a season.

Eventually, the cut of my trousers was everybody's small talk, everybody's jest.

So for my vacation I stayed far from them in the unthinkable Palace Hotel in Kansas, where the doorknobs were genuine crystal, where during winter months, the domestic help spoke only an antique Arabic, and where in the still wake of overwhelming ice storms red-tailed squirrels could be collected out on the grounds, with a varnish of ice a quarter-inch thick. In fact, as I write this, now, a tender scarlet tanager defrosts in my hand. I wonder if, when he is completely thawed, he will lay limp in my hands like a lovely sad cloth, or if he will sit up and sing and louder sing in praise of Kansas's brittle winter landscape?

* * *

And stay I did for weeks and months, in love with that easeful winter clarity until, one morning toward spring, I awoke in Simon Fish's luxury accommodations feeling less than enthused, feeling less than I had every right to feel given the first class considerations I was putting up. In a hotel that promotes itself as a "dream-of-perfection-come-curiously-true-in-Kansas," I think one has a right to expect that everything (including what may elsewhere in the world be referred to as "moods") be utterly provided for. At any rate, I woke feeling like my suite was trying to excrete me. I stumbled in pajamas toward the door, but found that it was stuck tight, as if there were a sphincter muscle in the door jamb. I babbled loudly for some of the Arab boys to come help.

I heard their cleverly slippered feet beating lightly outside the door, then the excited rattle of them trying to organize. At last, with a vapid pop, the door gave. Three or four of the boys lay discharged on the floor. I stepped past them in an awful hurry, disgusted. I ran through a labyrinth of lavishly tiled intestines, looking for the front door.

When at last I found myself outside on the front steps of the hotel, I realized that the impulse to leave my room had been providential. It was meant that I should see something amazing. Off to the northwest of the Palace, approaching without a sound (in fact, approaching in a silence that would have panicked me in a moment less divinely directed), was a dark, boogery, shitten ocean that crested hundreds of feet in the air. I'd been forced from the trivial and mendacious microintestines of the hotel so that I might see, be caught up in this enormous bowel of dust. God's great intestine, funnelling down the high plains, beginning with a gentle push in Bismarck, smirching the Dakotas, leaving sullied a crabbed corner of Nebraska, fouling with an arid debris northeastern Colorado, finally achieving with real force without extenuating interceding punctuation God's own country the great high plains wheat's home Kansas. (Yes, Arkansas, Oklahoma, and New Mexico would feel its filthy wrath next. But who cares about what happens in states the whereabouts of which one is so uncertain? A hundred thousand people will die in China today, too. Yucatan will experience a plague of frogs. A Parisian will find that his croissant was made with rancid butter.

Sand fleas will give Ethiopians a terrible itch.)

I rushed for a tractor and drove out, beyond the sanctuary of Simon Fish's hotel, to meet the sooty Godsend. As I came very close, the tiny and terrible dust devils began sweeping in their milling hundreds by my less and less massive tires. I got off the tractor and took shelter in one of the empty farmhouses that were strewn about Morton County. (I resist the idea that anyone ever lived in them. You know, it's pure folly, New Deal sentimentality, to pretend that every pathetic, poorly shingled, paintless and preposterous homestead shack is the key to some sad tale that would strike deep if we but knew it. Those doors that the wind bangs so freely are not mouths. They cannot speak.)

Whatever the case, I was glad for somewhere other than outside to be as this huge blow worked itself up. Inside, there was actually an unsteady, crude oaken table and a caned chair to sit in. I made myself comfortable but kept my eye on the storm. I took an old, chipped, grainy tea cup in my hand and felt brave enough to watch what was coming.

Well, I'm here to tell you that that old duster came up and sat down in my very front yard. It gyrated, stomped, buzzed and bored. It filled my mouth so I could not speak. Filled my nose so I could hardly breathe. But I think it wanted me to see, just as Yahweh wanted Moses to see. That was no dust storm. It was Theos asserting a constitutional obligation. This was God's own personal *jihad*.

As I watched, I saw this dust storm, with malice for no

one, concerned only with truth, sit and turn in the yard, peeling away by careful degrees layers of sand and dirt. Objects began to surface. First, the bruised, abraded rubber head of some little girl's baby doll. The flap top then the whole box of Wheat Krispies (including an offer of a free cereal bowl to anyone who'd like one for ten cents). The wind worked away at the sand, revealing oil cans, axles, steering wheels, sparrows, radio tubes, dime novels, a board with the dry rot, "I seen our wheat dry up and blow over the fence," a dead chicken in the mouth of a dead fox, no roots, a bean for dinner, the word *DROUGHT* scratched into the cover of a Bible, a laugh so bad it couldn't say "America," Kodak film at thirty cents per roll, "You and me, brother," "A piece of meat in the house would like to scare these children of mine to death," a farm boy who got his ears lowered, a hard get-by, the milk cow that went dry in '32, the coil from Uncle Josh's still, the unkindness of a federal agent, the tour of a tourin' car, the blade of an old plow, the scent of its mule, a cross of sticks for her sixteen-year-old son who died of cholera half-way to Oregon, a pioneer wagon wheel, an Indian camp ground, an Indian's bones, an entire burial grounds, rattles, arrow heads, jewelry, a branding iron, a Spanish stirrup, the fossilized remains of a giant sloth, the morose depth of a billion years of indifferent rock.

* * *

As I sat powerfully impressed by this grainy revelation, the filthy china cup still locked in my fingers, I received a visitor. Pacing through the broken front door, comfortable as you please, was our *padrone*, Simon Fish. He walked with an arthritic stiffness, unless it was just a matter of his being an American primitive. He came over to me and said, "The land is defiled; the land itself vomiteth out her inhabitants. Don't it?"

I said nothing, so he pulled up a busted oak chair and sat across from me. Suddenly, this was sacred space, cleared for the proper rendering of a sublime Figure.

"I don't suppose I've told you the legend of Murphy Holler, have I?"

"No, I don't suppose you have."

"Well, sir, it's one peculiar story. It so happens that I was there to see it all transpire, being the deputy sheriff of Identity, Kansas at the time. Luke they called me, back in my sheriffin' days."

I remembered, then, Simon Fish's reputation for untruth. I'd heard that he'd been called "Tyrone" at the time, and that he spent a lot of nights drinking cough remedy, or paint remover, or Dr. Sass's pure tonic, and screamin' up and down the town. But for the purposes of this story, "Luke" it was.

"Back in those days we had a spring like this one, dust and wind. But we didn't know who or what was responsible till one afternoon this fella Murphy Holler come a'saunterin' into town from the west, headin' a contradictory east, and chilling a fine Kansas day. How we suffered for his presence, innocent though he seemed! But a few of us, notably the Reverend Phenues Boyle and the oil man Carl Weather, discovered what he was about: Wobbly abominations! Sexual perversions! Boyle and Weather helped us to set things right. For it *was* confusion."

Unfortunately, the howling of the wind, clawing at the fabric of our little house, made the storytelling that followed often sound like nothing more than a dog barking. Nonetheless, I heard most of it, and what I heard was elemental and potent. So, here it is, here is the Legend of Murphy Holler.

* * *

Well, friend, Simon began, now you know what it's like to be overrun by a giant duster. It's like being overtaken by an entire, impetuous ocean. Only here, as you can see, there's no way to bubble safely to the surface. The closest breath of fresh air is hundreds of feet up. Man, you may as well be at the very bottom of the very blackest sea with ugly, eyeless dinosaur fish, creatures that prowl in a trifling darkness, whispering.

But these storms are no better for those who manage to get indoors. I mean, it is just as frightening. Folks at home wet towels to stuff window sills to keep the dust out. Then they pace the floor with a damp cloth over the mouth, a moan stuck in the throat, and an uneasy but constant desire to look out to see if the bad man, the mammoth Sand Man has come yet. When they look out the window, there it is—a towering red wall moving forward. It's eerie because there isn't even much wind— the wind is behind the dust cloud, moving it. The red dust is Oklahoma dust, a red clay common there. But

Oklahoma is two hundred and more miles away. It's then they realize that this cloud won't pose all day picturesquely in the distance. It, like an unwanted stranger, is passing through. Maybe he'll spend a night, maybe two. And maybe he'll decide he likes your little town.

After one such storm, the southerly winds dropped as suddenly as they had come, and the fine particles began to settle. Out at the Cricket Luncheonette, where I had taken refuge, we sat in our dusty chairs and watched the fertile fog sink slowly and silently, covering everything—including ourselves—in a thick blanket. Then, at last, we noticed things again. We noticed that our hair had gone gray and stiff and that we were grinding dirt between our teeth. These were the signs that we had been buried for the last few hours, and that only now were we rising from our graves.

Following the dust came 'hoppers, droning out of the southwest. Like the dust storms, they formed a dark cloud on the horizon, although it was not nearly so high. This one was lower and a little lighter, and because of the bug-to-bug makeup of the thing it shifted noticeably from side to side. But it was a sight that made the dusters seem friendly.

Well, lordy, man, I'm tellin' you, those 'hoppers were hungry. There weren't but six or seven blades of grass left behind by the dust storm, so after those were chawed down, those pests had to find something else to eat. So they ate Mrs. Amos's laundry, and they ate farmer John

James's every other fence post. They ate the hair off a dog. They ate the tires off a Studebaker. They ate the Sears catalogue at the P.O. They ate the dividing line on the main highway into town. They ate a blue streak. They ate the fancy-pants hat off a Johnny-come-lately. They ate our common purpose, community resolve, what we gave at the office, our best selves, and our sense of decency. When they had gone, we were left the poorer, there's no doubt.

It should not come as any surprise to you that we Kansans were not used to being so helpless before our problems. We sent our sons to fight for democracy in President Wilson's war to end wars. We won that same war with wheat, and damned if we didn't work by lamplight if need be to get the crop in. But how does a man stand up to dust and bugs? There wasn't one of those 'hoppers a two-year-old couldn't have skooshed beneath his foot. So what could we do? What way was there for us to show what we were made of?

It's with this as a background that I come to the most misunderstood episode in the history of Kansas in the mid-thirties: our Sunday rabbit drives. For whoever it was causing all our trouble, dust and voracious insects weren't enough. Scouring behind the grasshoppers, combing the plains, drawing the line nowhere, came rabbits.

Now, I know what you have read, mister, in every milk-hearted, cereal-minded, Kansas-hating Eastern newspaper. There we were: dirt farmers, clobber boys, up to our waists in cute cotton-tails, beating them right and left without method or the benefit of scientific investigation. We beat them over the head or whatever other part of their frantic bodies we could apply a Louisville Slugger or the bald-headed end of a broom to.

But there was good reason for our malice. You know we didn't have anything left in our fields. We had our canned goods and the little money in our bank accounts. But we still had to feed our stock. In and around our barns was hay from the last few years which we hoped would serve this purpose. So, you can imagine how a farmer felt when he saw his haystack moving, shimmying. A haunted hay pile? So, he'd send old Mose to investigate. As soon as Mose got a whiff of that hay and let out one loose bay, the stack seemed to disappear as a thousand gray fleeing rabbits bounded off. The rabbits ate a lot of what little there was, but—much worse than that—they fouled what they didn't eat. A cow would starve before it would touch that hay. Only one crittur would eat it now: another rabbit. And we weren't just all that interested in herdin' bunnies.

Now, the scientists that the federal government sent to us explained that the "jackrabbit population" had "proliferated" because the drought improved "breeding conditions." (Which means that none of their vermin young drowned in their damned dens.) Others said the jackrabbits migrated into Kansas in search of grass. But there weren't none of those scientists around when a milling dust storm would come through actually spawning rabbits in its folds. I've seen this with my own eyes and know it to be a fact. It is in no way natural for there to be so many thousands of rabbits. The explanation that we were all convinced of was that the rabbits were actually bred by and in the dust: Any fool could see them sprinting from the dirty, motherly pleats.

And so we had no compunctions. These were in no way God's creatures. That's why it was fitting, of a Sunday, to gather for a rabbit drive. Each week the citizens of our community would meet at a different local farm. Some of us would join hands in a huge, solemn circle that might be over a mile in diameter. Others of us would bang pans or cause our horses to snort. As we walked toward the center, our walls getting denser and denser, the rabbits ran before us. Finally, the rodents were driven into pens where the beaters would have at them. I've still got memorabilia from those drives: pictures of the rabbits thick as a carpet, the beaters knee-deep in jackrabbit panic, the crowd all around the pen like a victorious army. And, of course, I still have some rabbit's feet and silky ears to put a chain through and give to any youngster who comes to see me.

I'm trying to say that we had nothing to be ashamed of in killing those rabbits. We needed to do it to save our meager crops and stock. These were not cute cottontails, but the Devil's own thumping, awkward jackrabbits. Destroying them brought us together as a community and gave us a sense of group purpose. We felt a lot better about it than we did about trying to step on a lot of grasshoppers. It made us healthy.

The only episode that I have to wonder about now is the tale that got told and often repeated about Murphy

Holler, one of the first instances of his "difference." Now, I can't claim any firsthand knowledge here. I didn't see any of it. But every other Identitite claims to have either seen it or to have a strict understanding. After a rabbit drive, Murphy Holler was seen carrying a lame rabbit in his arms up to his room. Now that in itself is not very hard to believe. Individually, there was something woeful and sympathetic about the rabbits. But an angry farmer who had heard about the rabbit-lover decided to "take matters into his own hands." He marched up to the boarding house and snapped open the door. Well, the story is that the rabbits just fell all over him. The story is that some of 'em flew spook-like through the door. The air was white with rabbit, the house pestilent. This seemed evidence to many of a great guilt. The farmer babbles about it to this day out at the state home.

* * *

Well, many of us were willing to let such incrimination go by. Who were we to pass judgment? It was all hear-tell anyway. But there were some among us who, for good or bad, felt they saw things more clearly. One such was the Reverend Phenues Boyle. Now, the people of Identity followed and respected him, but that isn't to say that they were at ease with him. For he was one of those who could approach the most virtuous bride, splendid in her whites, and, holding his hand to her cheek, catch in his palm the twisting worm of atrocity as it tumbled from her curls.

Boyle knew about Holler and he knew about the rabbit

story. So no one was surprised when, before long, Mr. Murph was the single subject of Boyle's sermonizing.

"My beloved neighbors," he began, "sinners." A big pause here. "Harvest time is almost here. But when your husbands, sons, and brothers go out to their fields this year, what is it that they shall reap? Dust! Dryness! Withered life! And what will you do about it? Stop your sinning?" Slow nod of the head. "Sure enough. That's a start. Stop the sinning for certain. Stop the drinking, and the gaming, the cursing and the loose talk. You young'uns, don't think about dancing, don't think about rubbing together your dry, lascivious thighs. Because in God's sight it is but the rasping of dead stalk against dead stalk!

"Friends, for years I been tellin' you about this Second Coming. I told you He wasn't goin' to stand your sinful living for too long. How could he abide *The Jack Benny Show* and V-8 Fords? This was all bound to happen. The first time, the Lord God in his mighty and righteous wrath sent a flood. This time he's sendin' the opposite—original dirt. Children, this is ultimate darkness. So must come the end of the world. He's going to pile it on. He ain't gonna give no pause. By the end, we all of us gonna be one full mile down, and upstairs a new garden starts, feeding on our justly corrupting bones. New grass, new trees, children, new ponds, new and cleaner fish for the sea. Folks, it's going to be some kind of wonderful. Full of His grace.

"But I ain't gonna be there, and you ain't gonna be there. We'll just be the crime, the ugliness that that beauty will be an answer to. So, what I'm saying, Kansans, is: Don't wait for this 'weather' to break, no spring is coming, this is a nightmare that will never end. Because this is *the* end. His end. Believe it."

You can imagine how the people of Identity took this. They weren't feeling too good about the dust to begin with. But now to find that the dust was their fault and their sin, well, it took the heart out of 'em. We all looked up to the Reverend with grief on our faces. Strangely, his own face seemed to be accumulating bruises. It was dark and splotched with blue. He continued.

"But there's one thing, Identites, that I haven't told you. I haven't had the heart for it. Nonetheless, as the Lord our Saviour our Benefactor our Bounteous Grace Giver and general Healer, Jesus Christ, is my witness, it's true. The fact is this: Before the Day of Judgment, before the return of His only son bearing a sword of dust, He'll give us one last chance. Or, rather," Phenues said, looking deep into each of our souls, "He has given us one last chance. The Lord God is always ready to test, even when the facts are beyond doubt. He's sure of the results already, bein' God and all, but He gives us foolish unbelievers one more try. And it's a big one.

"What the Lord has done is this: He has sent the very Devil himself into our midst. Beelzebub, the Black One, lives in our bosom. Now if we spurn him and cast him aside, we pass the test. We are graciously given a little longer to linger on the good green earth. But if we mess up, if we sing and dance with the devil, and give him a bottle of Budweiser and a chicken salad sandwich and let him sleep in our homes . . . why, then, folks, it's the end of the . . ."

At just that moment, the Reverend Boyle was startled by something at the rear of the hall. It was Murphy Holler, leaning up against the wall, behind the very last pew. This was apparently the right moment for him to declare his presence, because he started walking up the aisle, a little cloud of dusty dirt hovering like a menace about the cuffs of his pants.

"You dare enter the House of the Lord, Satan-spawn?" asked Boyle.

"I think I'd better dare that and a good deal more if I mean to stay alive, Reverend." Holler had reached the front of the church and he turned to face the nearly overwhelmed audience. Tanned, wearing jeans, boots, and a working shirt open at the neck, he looked like the hero out of a kind of movie we hadn't seen yet. It was more drama than a fair number of faint Identity hearts knew how to handle. Except one. For up behind Holler crept the oil man Carl Weather, glowering, putting off a good amount of heat. Boyle and Weather between them created a glow at Holler's back that you might say was like a halo if you didn't know it was awfully God danged different, if you didn't know it was meant to consume him whole.

Now, Murphy Holler wasn't a big man. He stood only about five-foot-six and weighed maybe a hundred-and-thirty-five pounds. Physically, he wasn't anything to worry a Kansan. On the average, he was just a boy to most of us. Heck, most of our women were bigger than he was. But there was something else about him. It was the look in his eye, the tautness of his muscles, the unpredictability of his curly briar of light brown hair. And, what maddened us most, he had a knowin', devilish sort of smile.

Then Holler said, "Reverend, what you say has got some truth in it, even if I'm no ways involved. These here dust storms are caused by sin, but it's sin against the land. The land is overworked, misused. And you're right about another thing, Jack Benny and the V-8 Ford is at the bottom of it. 'Cause you folks can't have Jack Benny and you can't have no Ford machines unless you have cash. And you can't have cash unless you have a cash crop. King wheat. So you plow up every square foot of Kansas that isn't under water or hasn't got a house on it. But if the rains don't come, the wheat won't hold, and, folks, if the wheat don't hold, these millions of acres planted with your hopes for Philcos and Coca-Colas and vacuum cleaners are about as solid as the seas."

He continued righteously. "And if it's a matter of people ain't been livin' right, like Reverend Boyle says, it's because people been robbin' each other with fountain pens, and guns, and havin' wars. Some of us are about to starve while others spend $5,000 on a little party. So, yes, it's come time to cross the river, but you got to know which river."

Well, Phenues Boyle was just rearin' back ready to launch another attack on the reasonablest devil any of us had ever heard (although he made us feel as conscience-bitten as Boyle had), when something more than unexpected happened. Something fell heavily out of the sky crashing through the great window behind Boyle. It was a gull, dead and there for all of us to see. "A SIGN!" bellowed Boyle, pointing with an awful, swollen finger. The gull, in hitting the ground, had split open. And from its enormous, bulging stomach wriggled and bounced thousands of teeming locusts.

Yep, a sign. Sure enough, a sign.

* * *

And then there was Carl Weather, owner of Weather Oil and Gary Cooper seem-alike, who has gone down in legend as Boyle's right hand man. Well, a lot of fine things have been said about Weather, and maybe he's earned them all, but let me tell you that this Weather article was not strictly the straight-shooter he wanted to seem. If his blue-burnt auto was his Desire, watch out!, it had no neutral, no reverse, no remorse, no "off" on the ignition switch, no foot brake, no hand brake, just a break-your-back if you're fool enough to get in the way. He liked oil only because he liked money, and he liked money only because he liked the heft of meat. T-bone steak in the hand, porterhouse in the palm, rib-eye, sausage links, a man's top-heavy leaning prick-piece, a woman's heavy hind-hunks, her bangable rear-quarters. That's what he liked, this crowd-pleaser, this posse-buster. And if you can't believe this of an oil man, stand around the butcher's case when they get out of their offices at five o'clock. First they look at the ground round and disdain it although the bloody mottle of the fat and meat mash gets them excited. Then they turn to the beef slabs. Not the roasts with which their wives will have to fiddle all day, but the pure, prairie-flat, topsoil-deep cuts of steak. Sear that over some charcoal, just enough to singe the hide, and it's a meal that makes them glad to have a pocket full of legal tender.

There was a lot more those honest Americans, Carl Weather's townspeople, didn't know about him. Did they know that when he was a boy he pushed a lawn mower over a puppy? Did they know that he deliberately rolled that tragic rattler inside Mrs. Olga Fever's newspaper? Did they suspect his lifelong veneration for the thrust of his own cock? Could they dream that he hated women who spoke their minds? Would they believe that at age fourteen he fathered a child in Mrs. Randolph Dew, the visiting aunt of Ricky Dew, a high school chum?

Now, mister, during this time Carl Weather had a girl friend, his secretary, as it happened, one Miss Jenny Lamp, whom he spread over nearly every piece of office furniture he owned, covering in addition the majority of client dossiers and charging the room with his peculiar heat. Lord, if an accountant had gotten near his books then, if he'd gotten his nose (for one reason or another— let's say he was checking closely a smudged figure) near enough to one of Weather Oil's special leather files, he'd have caught his breath, stared dumbly, conjured an amazing scene, and said, "No, the idea is absurd." Nevertheless, he'd have had to take an early lunch. For the deep smell of Jenny's musk, locked in the pores of the leather, would unnerve him.

On some days, Carl would come in and close himself into his office in order to be alone with his lusts past and present. Once, he pressed his nose to the seat of the chair where Jenny took dictation. And then he saw her everywhere, stockings rolled down to her ankles, skirt pinned up above her hips, draped over a chair, perched on a filing cabinet, fallen over his desk. He sat behind that same desk, covered his eyes with a strong hand, and began weeping, the soft weeping changing slowly to sobs that racked and stretched him. All of a sudden up his belly crept a monster, wedging its keen reptile's head between his belt and belly. He called for Jenny and said, "Help me, Miss Lamp, help." The flared, scarlet head climbed above his belt as if it were an exotic but poisonous amphibian, a deadly sort of chameleon that was about to escape its cage. And Jenny said, "Oh, my poor Carl, my poor little baby. Does it hurt too much?" And she foolishly took the dragon by its neck as if it were nothing more dangerous than a little blue-belly and stroked it until its beastly sternness dissolved.

And then what gratitude, what kisses, what presents he gave to her. But she was only concerned that he feel better and stop crying. At last he did feel better, and he could do a little work, make a phone call, put a stamp on an envelope, use his stationery for writing a letter. But not long after lunch, just a few hours after the last outburst, in the depth of his trousers he felt a sinister prowling. And he knew that soon, in terror and panic, he would have to appeal to Jenny to come to his aid, to help him, to be kind to him, just a little.

* * *

It was these three—Boyle, Weather, and Lamp—that had the big parts to play on the Last Day.

The day of our atonement or the day of our great sin didn't start out as anything special for me. I woke early and groggy and so made my pot of coffee extra black. I had just stumbled over to the sheriff's office with my thermos of devil's drink and had barely had time to stretch my legs up on the desk when in the front door rushed Carl Weather with a leather portfolio of some kind under his arm.

"What's the matter, Carl?" I said.

Well, he couldn't get it out right away. He sorta looked around, made a few peculiar noises with his tongue, ran a hand over his unshaven chin. At last he looked me dead in the eye and said, "It's this here file, Deputy."

"Well, what is it, Carl," I said, leaning over curiously, picking the thing up, heavy and moist.

Weather just wasn't going to get it out real quick. He sorta sputtered, "It's some facts, Luke."

"I can see that, Carl. But why do you bring them to me?"

Suddenly Weather turned a good deal ferocious. He smacked his hand down on that file of his so hard it made my desk boom. "I got the facts and figures right her. Alls I want is for you to do your job and arrest that man Holler. I'll press the charges."

"Fine, you want me to arrest him," I echoed, now more

than a little troubled by the drift of things. "But for what?"

"For bein' a Wobbly, that's for what. For practicin' abominations. For bein' the cause of a general misery. All that's for what. He's left a trail of socialist trouble through Idaho, Montana, and Colorado which you could uncover easy as a blue tick hound can track a pork chop if you cared to."

It's hard to say no to a guy like Carl Weather. I sure didn't know how at that moment. He said he had the goods on Holler. Beats me if he did or not. I flipped through those papers of his, some of 'em signed by Oregon logging officials. Looked as much like the crosswise scrapings of a bunch of crickets as they did anything else. But, let me tell you, it was no time to cross Carl Weather. I could tell he had a purpose. So I said, "Tell you what, Carl. I'll bring Holler in for questioning until I can have someone from the state take a look at these here facts."

"Good enough for me, Deputy," he replied.

I got up slowly and strapped on my revolver. Don't know why I did that. It felt like everyone in town was looking at me while I took off my pants. I guess I did it because Weather seemed to want me to. He seemed to expect a whole lot of me that morning.

We stepped outside and the morning sun was close to blinding. It was then I noticed two other things. One, from the west was coming a gentle breeze on which fell a black drizzle, a powder-fine, charcoal dust. I guessed that another storm was kickin' up. The other thing I noticed, much blacker than the sooty air, was the figure of Phenues Boyle, dressed in his pitchy vestments and his three-corner hat just like it was Sunday or some other dark occasion. He grinned and that about frightened me to death.

"Now, dang it, Weather, what's he doing here?" I complained.

But Carl Weather was done talking. "Let's go," was all he felt like saying. And they were off, Weather, Boyle, and a number of others. I could follow or I could stay behind. At that point it didn't seem to matter much to them.

I knew I should have been leading this thing, not dragging behind, so I tried to run but I couldn't ever quite catch up. The best I could do was scamper at their hem, nip at the flanks, all with the effectiveness of herding jackals. Whatever the case, I was looking at Weather and Boyle's backs all the way to Holler's rooms. By that time it was pretty clear that I was plainly not leading an official party, under oath, performing a duty; I was trying to get control of a mob.

When we got to the door, I did manage to struggle to the front. So when Carl opened the door, I was among the first to see inside. And what a powerful eyeful I got. There in the middle of the floor was little Murphy Holler without a stitch on, just rubbin' all over Carl Weather's girl, Jenny Lamp.

Well, you can imagine, when ol' Murph saw us he next to had a fit. He jumped to his feet and the blood drained from every part of him except this prod, this lengthy stave which stood out before him. We looked at that thing and just sort of stared. I think most of us forgot for a moment why we were there. I know I did.

At last it was Lem Snicker said something, in the voice of the recently skeptical now true-believer: "Would you look at the billy on that guy! My God, I do believe he is the very Devil!"

Then it was that Carl Weather and Reverend Boyle remembered what they were about. "Rape!" roared out Weather. "Kill the Devil," shouted Boyle. And then they charged.

But Holler was quick. He launched himself headfirst out a window. He hit the ground, rolled once, and started sprinting, a spray of his own hot blood behind.

Well, some of those boys started after Holler, but I was too amazed at what was happening to get involved in the chase. Weather, too, stayed behind. I thought he was going to tend to his employee, Miss Lamp, who was still on the ground sorta writhing and moaning. Weather was saying something to her and kind of kickin' her with his boot. It was a strange way to bring a savaged girl about. He'd mutter something, then give her a little shot in the ribs. I began to suspect that Murph Holler wasn't the only surprised man in town.

For one reason and another, I let a lot of things happen that day that maybe I oughtn't have. I won't say my performance was without fault. But I wasn't about to let Weather carry on in this vein for long. So I gave him a shove in the chest (amazing how good that felt) and said, "That'll be enough, Carl. Don't be doin' her like that."

Jenny preferred silence. She pulled herself up and put some clothes on. She had nothing to add to what we'd seen with our own eyes. For me, though, her face seemed a little softened and saddened, with maybe a little tear tucked into the corner of one eye. Whatever had been going on, one thing's for sure: Weather and Miss Lamp were never again the hot number they had been.

By the time I caught up with that mob, they were clustered and buzzing around the home of the widow Edna Robins. Apparently that's where old Murph had gone to take refuge. There must have been some suspicion that he had managed to find a gun as well, 'cause no one was making any motions toward the front door. Instead folks were just shoutin' out, "Mad dog!" and "Surrender!"

Of course, I was more worried about what this crowd was going to do than I was worried about Holler. If I'd just had a few more minutes, I do believe I could have persuaded the majority of them to go on back home. But I think poor Murphy was a little frantic, 'cause it wasn't long before he made a sprint for it, out the back door, down an alley, firing shots in the air.

But nothing, not even bullets, was going to distract those people that morning. They let out a howl of rage and disappointment and took after him with clubs and some guns of their own. They ran till everyone was near exhausted. They sprinted down to the slippery banks of the Identity River. Murphy even tried to get across. But when he got up to about his chest, he realized that the current was too strong to swim, so he turned on his attackers and delivered an ultimatum.

"This is it, folks! Not another step or one of you is dead. This ain't no joke."

But no one was laughing. Those people were in a rage and in no mood to stop. Twenty or thirty of them plunged into the river. It must have been a hell of a scarey sight for Holler, those heavy bodies falling toward him. So he took aim and fired the gun. You might have guessed it, that fool Lem Snicker took a shot in the chest and fell face down in the Identity River, dead as a clam. Holler had one more bullet and he winged Jeremy Bottle, our town barber. After that they swarmed on him. All I could see was that thatch of curly brown hair tossing up and down. You might have thought he was a queen bee if you didn't know better.

I'm just not gonna deal much with what they done to him. Even this many years after the fact, I don't have the stomach for it. But I will say that they bared his flesh like they bare the earth each spring, and then, at the Reverend Boyle's instruction, they beat him with the branches of a wild fig. Next, they carved on him a bit after which he really was more dead than alive. Then they took him to the U.S. route 54 overpass, put a rope around his neck, and strung him up high and proper. Looking up at Holler, God knows what leaking from his body, the Reverend Boyle proclaimed, "Divine wrath is appeased."

And just two little days later came a benediction from Governor Graff, a statement praising the lynching as "a lesson to every state in the union."

* * *

Hearing the legend of Murphy Holler capped my stay at the utopian Palace Hotel, dream-place of Simon Fish, Kansas Wheat King. My supervisor, the Vice President of the Perusal of Etc. was now sending me threatening cables and attempting to place hostile long-distance calls. He was hauling me back to Hartford, headquarters, headwaters, heartburst. I was ready to go home anyway.

Simon had one of his staff arrange for all the travel particulars, so when he stood at the pale blue front doors of his now enormously successful hotel and handed me the ticket and itinerary which would send me racketing home on a Santa Fe Zephyr—all that was left for me to do was to take the enormous man into my arms, hug him, and fight back the painful tears. "Oh, Simon Fish, never, never will I forget you," I said. "And I'll be back, I'll be back," I choked, limping down the long cement walk to the limousine that was to take me to the station. I don't expect you to believe it of such a great man, but I do believe that there was even a little tear in the corner of each of Simon's eyes.

Yes, we had grown to be like brothers. Which is a way of saying that my stay in Morton County, Kansas, had brought about deep and abiding changes in me. On these I reflected during the long trip home. Up in the scenicruise dome I'd sit, a copy of *Life* magazine spread on my lap, Missouri, Illinois, Indiana, Ohio, Pennsylvania all passing before me. I had time to reflect that now I, like fabled Diamond Jim Brady, was reclining in a train, in comfort if not luxury, whipping over the belly of the vast U.S.A. I could almost see him across from me, commanding a row of seats, proprietorial, masterful, a confident look in his eyes, a cigar burning like incense in one of his massive hands. He looked at me meaningfully, his diamond stickpin flashing. "Well, what's it going to be, son?" he asked. "How are you going to have it now? Have you got what it takes? Are you afraid of success? Do you want that car, those servants, that house, hell, that estate? Or do you just want some papers to push and some guy who makes you call him 'Mr.,' who comes in and lays his dick on your desk?" He laughed his deep, chesty laugh—a-haugh-haugh—and made the end of his cigar glow like the sun.

Then up the corridor, ambling slow, like he was looking for a seat where the conductor wouldn't see him, came Murphy Holler. He had a guitar and some rags on his back, his hands in his pockets, a "Buddy, can you spare a dime" on his lips. But there was also that Hollerish look in his eyes, that knowing insolence. He looked at Diamond Jim and he looked at me and passed on to the next compartment.

I guess you could say I'd made up my mind, made my choice. They weren't going to know me back in Hartford. I was reconciled, I was ready now, I'd know what to do at garden parties. The next time I saw a wife at one of those, I'd push her head down in a bowl of champagne punch, and I'd wait until the bubbles were from her lungs. Then I'd mount her in full view, a message to all, don't tread on me, my now steel-tempered root, anaconda hard, dauntless, indomitable, ripping through the fabric of her dress, striking home, engendering.